Fear raged through Marielle.

This was the man who had attacked her at home...

The man pounded on the bedroom door. "Let me in!" The noise grew more intense. He was smashing the door with his body.

Ian gave a cry. Marielle wrapped his blanket around his shoulders and held him close. "It's okay. I've got you."

She flung the window open. It was a short drop down. Ian lifted his head, round brown eyes watching her. "I'll let you down, and then I'll come out right after you. Okay?"

Ian nodded.

A voice came from outside the window. "Hand him down to me." Graham. He had figured out what was going on.

The door began to splinter. Marielle helped Ian out, and Graham took the boy.

Her feet had just hit the snow when the door burst open. Still holding Ian, Graham tried to navigate around the deeper drifts. Marielle sought to step in the holes he'd made.

A shot rang out behind them. The man had a gun...

Ever since she found the Nancy Drew books with the pink covers in the country school library, **Sharon Dunn** has loved mystery and suspense. In 2014, she lost her beloved husband of nearly twenty-seven years to cancer. She has three grown children. When she is not writing, she enjoys reading, sewing and walks. She loves to hear from readers. You can contact her via her website at sharondunnbooks.net.

Books by Sharon Dunn

Love Inspired Suspense

Wilderness Secrets
Mountain Captive
Undercover Threat
Alaskan Christmas Target
Undercover Mountain Pursuit
Crime Scene Cover-Up
Christmas Hostage
Montana Cold Case Conspiracy
Montana Witness Chase
Kidnapped in Montana
Defending the Child

Alaska K-9 Unit

Undercover Mission

Pacific Northwest K-9 Unit

Threat Detection

Mountain Country K-9 Unit

Tracing a Killer

Visit the Author Profile page
at LoveInspired.com for more titles.

DEFENDING
THE CHILD

SHARON DUNN

LOVE INSPIRED SUSPENSE
INSPIRATIONAL ROMANCE

LOVE INSPIRED® SUSPENSE
INSPIRATIONAL ROMANCE

Recycling programs
for this product may
not exist in your area.

ISBN-13: 978-1-335-48402-4

Defending the Child

Copyright © 2025 by Sharon Dunn

Love Inspired
22 Adelaide St. West, 41st Floor
Toronto, Ontario M5H 4E3, Canada
www.LoveInspired.com

Printed in U.S.A.

To every thing there is a season,
and a time to every purpose under the heaven.
—*Ecclesiastes* 3:1

For my readers as always,
whose encouragement keeps me writing.

ONE

Marielle Coleman awoke to the sound of someone moving around in her house. The noises emanating from downstairs were muffled, and her first thought was that her four-year-old foster son, Ian, had crawled out of his bed and gone downstairs for a snack. Not something he had ever done before, but maybe he was starting to feel more comfortable here.

Her pounding heart told her something more sinister was taking place. Still listening, she sat up in bed and pulled back the covers.

Another noise reached her ears, a heavy boot tread on the floorboards, probably coming from downstairs. Her breath caught in her throat. She had not imagined an intruder. Someone was definitely in the house—and she had reason to be afraid. Ian was the only witness to a crime in which his mother, Kristen, had been killed and his father, David, had disappeared. Police believed that Ian had seen the man who killed his mother, but the boy had gone mute from the trauma. He could only nod or shake his head when asked questions. The police were not sure if the murderer knew Ian had witnessed the crime, but this home invasion confirmed that he had.

Her chest squeezed tight as she reached for her phone on the table by her bed and dialed 911.

The operator's crisp voice came across the line. "911. What is your emergency?"

"Someone's in my house, 1811 Maverick Lane. Hurry," she whispered and disconnected, not wanting any noise to cause the intruder to find her all the faster.

Still holding the phone, she bolted up

from the bed. After stepping into her slippers and grabbing her robe, she put the phone in her bathrobe pocket and rushed down the hallway to Ian's room. The glow of the night-light revealed a blond head and tiny arms that held a well-worn stuffed giraffe.

She touched his shoulder and whispered, "Ian, wake up."

The child turned over on his side but remained asleep.

More footsteps. The intruder was on the stairs. Panic threaded through her making her heart race. The police wouldn't get here in time. She lived fifteen miles from the nearest town.

She picked up the boy, taking his giraffe and blanket with her. Ian drew the stuffed animal closer to his chest and let out a tiny moan.

They could not leave by the front door without encountering the intruder. Holding Ian close to her chest, she hurried back to her room. She transferred him to one arm so she could grab the go bag she'd prepared for this possibility and pushed open the sliding glass door that led to a balcony and stairs. Cold air enveloped her as snowflakes landed on her face. Ian stirred against her, and she sped down the stairs.

Snow soaked through her slippers when she ran around to the front of the house where her car was parked. After tossing the go bag in, she placed Ian in his car seat in back and clicked him in. He was still half asleep.

She patted his arm and pressed her hand on his cheek. "There you go, little guy. Snug as a bug."

She turned her attention to the dashboard as a whole new level of terror sank in, taking her breath away.

The car keys were inside the house.

She straightened up and glanced down the lonely road at lights in the distance. It was too far to run to the neighbors. In slippers, the trek would be close to im-possible.

When she looked at the house, she saw a light flashing at a window on the second floor. The intruder was still searching up there. It would be only a matter of minutes before the culprit figured out how she and Ian had escaped. Her hands had been too full to close the balcony door, providing evidence of her escape route. All the intruder had to do was glance out a front window and see that she was by the car.

She had to get out of here and fast.

Rushing toward the front door, she tried to ignore how cold and wet her feet had become. Though she'd locked the door before going to bed, it opened when she twisted the knob. Her car keys were in a bowl on a table in the entryway. She grabbed the whole bowl. Her feet were frozen blocks by the time she made it back to the car. She swung the driver's door open, grabbed the keys and tossed the bowl on the passenger seat.

She shoved the key in the ignition and shifted into Reverse. Once she was turned around, Marielle switched on the headlights, revealing the long, snow-covered driveway and a sports car parked some distance from the house that must belong to the intruder. He or she must have walked the rest of the way to avoid detection.

Marielle pressed the gas and dared herself a look in the rearview mirror. A silhouetted figure, most likely male, stood in the downstairs doorway. The image sent chills down her spine, and she floored it. Five minutes later, the neighbor's house, shrouded in shadows, came into view. All the windows were dark. She remembered then that the Wallaces had gone on a two-week cruise. She wouldn't find refuge there. She headed toward the main road that would lead into the nearest town. Clarksville was fifteen miles away.

Snow flew across her field of vision, and she switched on the windshield wipers. She barely came to a stop at the crossroads before turning onto the paved road.

Shivering, she switched the heater on high, thankful for the warm blast that hit her face and feet. The snow was coming down hard enough to reduce visibility. She was grateful that her four-wheel drive could handle the slick roads.

She pressed her car through a series of curves. When the road straightened out, she saw a set of headlights behind her. Her grip on the steering wheel tightened.

That had to be the man who had invaded her home. No one else would be out at this hour in this kind of weather.

She could see Ian in her rearview mirror. He rubbed his eyes with a tight fist and looked around. She thought she read fear in his expression.

More than anything, she wanted to pro-

tect Ian's heart and mind. The child had
been through enough. Both his parents
had been drug users and low-level deal-
ers, though his mother had gotten sober
in the last months of her life.

She swallowed to try and erase the fear
from her voice. "It's going to be all right,
kiddo."

The other car loomed behind her, drawing closer.

She wasn't going to be able to shake
him.

The snow cleared momentarily, and she
saw the sign on the side of the road indicating that the next exit would take her
to the Bridger Bible Camp. The pursuer's car fishtailed on the icy road, and a
thought occurred to her. The man's car
was a low clearance sports car. She might
not be able to outrun him on the highway,
but he'd most likely get stuck or not be
able to traverse the mountain road that
led to the camp. Her four-wheel drive
would make it easily. She'd gone there as

a kid and a teenager and then worked as a counselor when she was in college. It also happened to be where she'd met the man she thought she was going to marry. Instead, Graham had broken her heart and left the state for a job as a DEA agent. But that wasn't important now. What mattered was that she knew the back way to get to the camp, and as far as she could remember, it was unmarked. So even if he followed her where she turned off the main road, he wouldn't know where she'd gone.

She drove past the Bridger sign and the road that led directly to the camp and kept going, scanning for where the unmarked access road was.

Without signaling, she waited until the last second to make the turn. The other car whizzed by. It would take the driver time to get turned around, if he dared try to follow her.

When she checked the rearview mirror, Ian had fallen back asleep.

Her vehicle scaled up the curving road until she came to where it split off. She turned, knowing that this would connect her to the road that led to the camp and hopefully conceal where she'd gone. She raced up to the top of a hill and turned a tight corner. Down below, the camp, with its large main meeting hall surrounded by smaller sleeping cabins and other buildings, came into view. A single lamplight provided enough illumination to show the outlines of some of the buildings and a snow-covered parking lot.

Snow was still twirling around her car as she headed downhill. If memory served, Adrian, the man who managed the camp, often had a caretaker stay on the grounds in the offseason. Perhaps she'd find some help here.

When she was nearly to the camp, she glanced in the rearview mirror. No headlights were behind her as far as she could see, and none were coming up the main road either. She'd lost her pursuer. When she looked ahead, she saw lights in the building beside the meeting hall.

She took in a deep breath.

Someone was here.

Though she was pretty sure she'd shaken the man in the car, this refuge would be temporary until the storm passed. If the intruder had been so bold as to break into her house, there was no telling what else he would do. No doubt, the culprit would come after Ian again.

When she pushed open the car door, a gust of wind and snow blasted her.

She trudged toward the warm glow of the light coming through the windows and pounded on the door.

Footsteps came from inside and then the door swung open.

"Please can you help me?" Her voice trembled as the wind whipped her long brown hair against her face. She hunched down against the cold. "I saw the light and hoped someone would be here."

"Sure, why don't you come in and get

warmed up? This storm is only going to get worse."

She picked up on the note of suspicion in his words. Understandable. She'd shown up at this out-of-the-way place dressed in pajamas and a robe.

"Thank you." She lifted her head to look at the man who was her impromptu rescuer. Shock spread through her. "Graham?"

"Marielle?" Graham Flynn felt like he'd been punched in the gut. Running into the woman he'd left ten years ago was not on his itinerary, especially not here, in the place where they'd first met. It was here they'd been campers and then counselors together, where they'd fallen in love, even where they'd chosen which college they'd go to together. And where he'd asked her to marry him.

It was a plan he'd been happy with, until he'd been recruited by the DEA. He hadn't realized before then how much he craved excitement and escape from small-town life. The work would take him all over the world. He'd asked Marielle if she was open to postponing the wedding or having a long-distance marriage for a few years. She'd said no. Marielle had dreamed of a quiet life in Montana raising a bunch of children and being a part of a small, close-knit community. She deserved to be with someone who could give her that. Given that he had grown up without a father, he thought he could do a lot more good in the world by becoming a law enforcement officer than a parent.

The last ten years of undercover work had made him feel like he was making a difference in stopping the drug trade. He was in his element and had found a vocation that fit his skill set. He'd thought the job was what he was meant to do—until the death of his CI a few weeks ago. He'd come up to the camp as a respite after sixteen-year-old Cesar had been murdered in a cartel explosion.

Perhaps the same memories of the camp were running through her mind as she narrowed her eyes and pinned him with her gaze. "I have to say. You're the last person I thought I would ever see again." Her voice had grown stronger as she lifted her chin slightly.

The tinge of anger in her words didn't surprise him. Choosing to ignore her emotional state, he took a step to one side. "Come in. You must be freezing."

She turned back toward the car. "I have someone with me." She descended the first step.

Her exposed ankles were red from the cold. "Let me help you."

"It's better if I do it," she said. "Ian is slow to trust strangers. I don't want him to get scared."

He grabbed his coat, which hung by the door, and followed her. As he bent over to shield his face from the wind, snow stabbed his skin like a thousand tiny swords. He watched as she reached into the back seat. She held a bundle beneath a blanket.

Of course, there was a child. There was probably a husband too. Had he thought time would stand still after he'd left town? He wondered, though, why she'd shown up here in such a state, dressed like she was, as if she'd fled a violent situation in the middle of the night. The thought of anyone hurting Marielle made him grind his teeth. Even after all these years, he still felt protective of her.

He closed the car door behind her and then followed her inside. "Why don't you two sit by the woodstove?"

He ushered them over to a love seat that was situated perpendicular to the stove and across from an overstuffed chair. The fire had nearly died out. He opened the door, stirred the coals and then threw on another log from the pile in the wood box.

She settled on the love seat and pulled back the blanket, revealing a blond boy of maybe three or four years of age. His cheeks were rosy. He stared up at Marielle while he clutched a worn stuffed animal. She stroked his head and made a shushing sound. "It's going to be all right. We're safe and warm now."

The boy rested against her chest.

Graham stood. "Your feet must be frozen." He went to the bedroom to retrieve a pair of his heavy wool socks from the dresser. Without thinking, he sat on the floor and pulled her wet slippers off. His fingers grazed over her skin. "Very red but doesn't look like you have frostbite."

She lifted her foot so he could put the sock on. "Your fingers are warm."

He pulled the sock up her ankle. "There you go."

"Thank you," she whispered as she looked at him. Her gaze softened. She still had the same long, wavy brown hair that had always made her so pretty. Eyes the color of dark chocolate only added to her beauty.

The look of appreciation in her face

made his heart beat a little faster. His face flushed. He cupped the other foot and slipped the sock on over her soft skin.

She stared at the fire through the glass window while he rose and grabbed a blanket from his bed to wrap around her.

"Thank you." She pulled the blanket tighter around her shoulders.

Clearly something bad had happened to her and he wondered if she'd share the details with him, but first he needed to get her warmed up. "How about I make you some hot tea?"

She continued to gaze at the fire. Her eyes were unfocused as she rocked the little boy in her arms. "That would be nice."

Her appearance suggested that she'd escaped some kind of violence. He only hoped that she hadn't brought trouble to his door. It wasn't just what she might be running from that worried him. Working undercover for the DEA meant he was always looking over his shoulder. The cartel had killed his informant with a car bomb. They could have just as easily figured out who Graham was and followed him up here.

The remoteness of the camp afforded a degree of protection to both of them because it was so hidden, but it also left them vulnerable if anyone knew where to find them. Cell phones did not work this high in the mountains, and the satellite phone was being repaired for when the camp was full of people. If danger found them, they were on their own.

He went to the kitchen and busied himself with the tea, trying to quell the rush of memories. Images of the time they'd spent together, of the kisses and the hikes and the long talks planning their life together, bombarded him, making him feel weak in the knees.

When he returned to where she sat, she'd laid the boy down on the love seat and covered him with the blanket.

He handed her the steaming mug. "What

brings you to this camp on such a snowy night?"

Marielle stared at him with a piercing gaze as his question hung in the air.

TWO

"I might ask you the same thing." Marielle looked at him over her cup of tea. "After all these years."

She was surprised by the sting in her words. Seeing Graham face-to-face after ten years brought back intense pain as if his rejection had happened yesterday. He'd chosen his job over a life with her.

Graham sat down in a chair that faced the love seat. "I needed some time off, and Adrian offered me time alone at the camp if I kept an eye on the place."

"Time off from what, exactly?" Her question sounded more like an accusation. Emotions that had been kept at bay for years assaulted her. At first after he left, she was devastated, but she'd gotten on with her life. She thought she'd healed. But now with Graham sitting only feet from her all the anger, hurt and confusion seemed to rise to the surface.

He averted his gaze. "You know, life, work, stress."

That sounded vague. There was probably more to the story. She shook her head. "After all this time. You came back and you didn't even get in touch with me?" Her words came out as if she were shooting them at him. Wasn't she at least owed that courtesy?

He leaned forward in his chair, pointing at the slippers on the floor. "You haven't told me what's going on with you and your son."

So that was his tactic, to change the subject. "Ian is my foster child."

His expression changed. The muscles in his face relaxed as though he was pleased by the news. "Oh, I thought…"

"I never married, and I don't have children of my own." After Graham's departure so close to their wedding, she'd poured herself into getting a master's in child psychology. She didn't want to date again and risk such unbearable pain. Her profession allowed her to help children if she was never going to have any of her own.

Graham rubbed his beard. "So why did you come here...tonight?"

He'd never been one to stop shaving. He looked different with facial hair. Still handsome but in a mountain man sort of way. His expression and especially his eyes held a tiredness that had not been there years ago.

She reached out to touch Ian's shoulder while the child slept. "This little guy witnessed a crime. Certain people may not want him to talk and identify them. Tonight, someone broke into my house, and I have to assume it's connected to Ian. When the intruder pursued me in his car, I had to shake him. That's why I came up here."

Graham jerked to his feet. "How do you know he didn't follow you here?" He seemed jumpy. Maybe it came with the territory when you were a DEA agent, but she doubted it.

Her eyes fell on the holster on his hip, which she hadn't noticed while he was seated. She gasped. "Graham, what is going on with you?" She pointed to the gun. "Surely you don't need that if you're taking time off?"

"Oh, it's just for protection, lot of wild animals out here." He was trying to make his voice sound casual, but she picked up on the tension underneath. He thought he needed protection even when he was hiding up here. Was she in some other kind of danger after escaping the intruder?

His explanation made no sense. He was carrying the gun on his person while he was inside. Besides, a rifle or shotgun would be better protection against wildlife. She had the feeling he was keeping something from her. Maybe his on-guard attitude wasn't just about her showing up here after being pursued.

Graham paced toward the window and looked out. "How do you know this is a safe place for you to bring Ian?"

She rose and stepped toward him. "I don't think the car the home invader was driving could make it up the back road. It was a low-clearance sporty-looking thing, probably rear-wheel drive. Plus, I took the unmarked road that leads up here."

"I remember that road." He ran his hands through his hair, something he always did when he was nervous. "What kind of crime are we talking about here?"

She glanced over to where the boy still lay asleep. Then she crossed her arms and turned to stare out the window before speaking in a low voice. "Ian witnessed someone kill his mother. He stopped speaking after it happened, but the police think he might be able to identify the murderer once he's able to talk. Both his parents were connected to the local drug trade."

"Why didn't you have a protection detail?" Graham asked, frowning in thought.

She sighed. This was a discussion she'd had with the police more than once. "Ian was probably hiding when it happened. Otherwise he might have been killed too. The police didn't think the killer had seen him and you know how small-town forces are. They couldn't extend the resources for protection unless they were sure it was necessary. I had a go bag just in case. Now I know that the killer knows. Whoever came after Ian tonight probably killed his mom."

Graham shook his head, clearly upset. "To go after a little kid like that…unbelievable." He looked at her. "Why was the mom killed?"

"Who knows? Life is cheap in that world. Maybe Kristen had drugs someone wanted or somebody thought she'd ripped them off."

"Was there a husband or boyfriend in the picture?"

She frowned. "A husband, David. Ian's father. He's missing, but police don't think he did it."

He met her gaze, and she thought she saw admiration in his eyes. "And now you're in the middle of this, taking care of the boy."

"I just want to protect an innocent life." When she stared out the window, the blowing snow nearly camouflaged her car even though it was parked only feet from the door. "You asked why I came here. I think this place always seemed like the safest place in the world to me. Maybe that's why I made the choice to come up the mountain."

He offered her a faint smile. "I always thought of the camp that way too. A refuge from life's struggles." Some light came into his eyes, reminding her of the Graham she'd known, not the world-weary one she was seeing now.

The moment of connection made her smile too.

Her heart fluttered when she met his gaze. The attraction was still there after all this time. She studied him for a long moment. The warm feelings faded when she remembered the pain he'd caused her, and she took a step back.

She'd given up trying to get a clear explanation from him why he'd come back after all this time. She had the feeling if she asked, he'd just continue being evasive.

He turned sideways so he could stare out the window, as if her looking at him had made him uncomfortable. "The storm's getting worse. No one is coming in or out until this lets up."

That meant she was stuck here with Graham while all the questions and intense emotions dancing in her head.

She returned to the couch to sit beside Ian, who stirred but did not wake up. "I'm just glad somebody was here." Though she wished it would have been somebody other than the man who'd torn her world apart.

"Why don't you and the little guy get some sleep?" He pointed toward the bedroom.

"I don't want to move him. It's warm and cozy by the stove," she said. "I can rest in the chair."

"Suit yourself." He handed her the blanket he'd draped over her earlier.

She drew the blanket up to her shoulders, grateful for it and the heat from the woodstove.

Graham wandered through the small manager's house, and she watched him check that all the doors and windows were secure. When he retreated to the bedroom, she noticed his hand resting on the butt of his gun. Maybe his training made him never let his guard down.

She closed her eyes and drifted off.

She awoke when Ian stirred, making a sound of distress. Was he having a bad dream or remembering something? She rose and stroked his head, making shushing noises. He cried for several seconds, and she took him into her arms.

"I've gotcha," she whispered as she swayed back and forth and then sat on the love seat. In the days since he'd been in her care, she'd discovered that he was responsive to touch and being held.

Kids who have come from physically abusive situations often bristled when touched. Someone had loved and protected Ian enough so he could be soothed despite his life circumstances. There were no grandparents in the picture, so she assumed his parents, despite their struggles, had taken care of him.

The boy quieted as she held him. After a while, she laid him back down on the love seat, making sure his blanket covered him.

She returned to her chair to sleep. Maybe the storm would keep the man who broke into her house at bay, but that didn't mean they wouldn't come for Ian again. She'd have to see if the sheriff's department could provide some protection once they got out of here now that it was clear the killer was after Ian. She closed her eyes and prayed.

God, keep this little boy safe and give me the strength to do right by him.

As she drifted off, she could hear Graham in the next room tossing and turning and then pacing. Was he as stirred up by her presence as she was about his or was it something else? The fact that he claimed to be taking time off but carried a gun scared her. He must have been worried about some kind of danger long before she'd shown up, and she doubted it was a bear or wolf.

Despite all her fear, or perhaps because of it, the fog of sleep invaded her mind.

She awoke with a start in the darkness, not sure how much time had passed. She could just make out Ian, a blanketed lump on the love seat. Still caught between consciousness and dreaming, she thought she heard a sound like a doorknob being rattled.

Heart pounding, she listened, but no additional noise reached her ears. She rose and walked toward the door, her footsteps silent in her borrowed wool socks. She touched the doorknob, but it was unmoving. Maybe the sound had been the wind.

She retreated back to the chair. Perhaps her fear of being found had caused her to dream that someone was trying to break in. She and Ian were trapped here until the storm lifted, and that was increasing her worries.

The last thing she heard before falling asleep was Graham moving through the house as if on patrol.

Actions that indicated he too was concerned that they were not safe.

A gust of wind rattled the glass of the window Graham gazed out of. He saw nothing but darkness outside, yet he could not let go of his unease. Snow still fell as if dumped from buckets.

Though his training made him vigilant out of habit, his need to detect and eliminate potential threats seemed to have ramped up since his informant's death. Cesar had been a sixteen-year-old kid who wanted something better for himself and his family. Undercover work was tricky. Even though you weren't supposed to form attachments, he'd begun to think of Cesar as a little brother.

His thoughts turned again to the events in Mexico that had brought him here. His handler didn't think there was anything he could have done to prevent the explosion that had killed Cesar. Graham felt, though, that he should have gotten wind of what the cartel had planned. That he should have known that Cesar had been outed as a CI. Had he not been careful enough when setting up their meetings?

He turned away from the window to

gaze at Marielle in the chair. She looked beautiful as she slept, her wavy brown hair falling across her cheek. Her showing up gave him even more reason for insomnia.

After all this time, she hadn't married. The thought made him sad. She'd always talked about having lots of kids. Being a mom had been her dream. By breaking up with her, he'd thought he had given her a chance at that dream.

The truth was, when the DEA recruited him, he'd thought he was doing her a favor. True, they were both Christians, but Marielle came from a stable family that had generations of faithful people. He'd grown up without a father and had only come to the Bible Camp as a teen to hide out before the police found out he'd stolen a motorcycle. The director of the camp that year had figured out what he was up to and had agreed not to call the police if Graham would stay at the camp all summer and commit to the activities.

He'd been well on his way to becoming a juvenile delinquent. Little did he know that his encounter with God at the camp would lead him to confess to the police and change the whole direction of his life.

Still thinking about the past, he returned to the bedroom. He sat down on the bed, resting his hands on his knees and running his palms over his head. The truth was, he'd thought Marielle deserved someone better than him, someone who could be a good husband and father. He feared he was not up to that task and that he could better serve God by chipping away at the drug trade.

He swung his legs onto the bed and pulled his covers up to his chin while he stared at the ceiling. Sleep came gradually.

Mindful of the need to stay on guard duty, he awoke hours later in the dark silence. He rose and peered out each window and checked that the door was locked. He looked out the front window where the snowfall had lightened up a bit.

He jerked his head back when he saw a flash of light. It was there and gone as though a curtain had been lifted and been pulled back down. He leaned toward the window.

Marielle appeared beside him. "What's going on?"

He hadn't even heard her padding across the floor, she walked so delicately. She stood close enough to him that her shoulder brushed against his.

"I thought I saw a light out there," he said.

She gasped. "Are you sure?"

He turned back toward the window, studying the area where he'd seen it before. "I'm not sure about what I saw." He moved to the other window and peered out, still searching.

Her voice feathered with fear. "Who would be out there?"

He wasn't about to tell her that the cartel may have found him. She had enough to worry about. "I heard someone built some vacation cabins a couple of hills over. I just can't imagine someone going out in this on purpose, unless they didn't realize the danger. Look, the darkness and the storm can play tricks on what you see."

Maybe he'd just imagined the light, a sort of winter mirage. His concern over intruders could make him see things that weren't there. He may have caused Marielle to be upset over nothing.

"I'm pretty sure that man's car couldn't make it all the way up the mountain. Even if he did, he would've had to guess at which way I turned." She rubbed her arms.

He put his hand on her shoulder, hoping his touch would help alleviate her fear. "We don't know anything for sure. Soon as this storm clears and the plows come, we can get out of here."

She studied him for a long moment. "But until then, we're stuck here, right?"

As he gazed into Marielle's brown eyes, he wanted more than anything to assure her that they were safe. But that would be a lie. He'd been fine when it had only been himself up here. If he was attacked by the forces that might be after him, he could take care of himself, but now he had a woman and child to think of.

"Tell you what. There isn't much of the night left. Why don't you and Ian go to the bedroom and get some sleep? I'll keep watch. This storm should let up by morning."

She nodded.

He watched her move to the couch and pick up the sleeping boy. At least he'd gotten a little rest. After the bedroom door clicked shut, he settled down into the chair that provided a view of the windows. He placed his gun on the side table.

For the next few hours, he stayed mostly

alert, nodding off from time to time and then rousing himself. Light streaming through the windows woke him for the final time. Morning finally.

Graham rose to his feet and stepped closer to the window. The sky was white. A milky film covered the sun, but the snowstorm had stopped.

Everywhere he looked he saw drifts. He was glad he'd parked his truck in the garage—Marielle's car was half covered in snow. He saw faint impressions in the snow that might have been footprints. The blowing and drifting made it hard to say. An animal could very well have wandered into the camp and made them. All the same, now that the storm had died down, he needed to do a search of the camp. In the calm daylight, they were more vulnerable. It would be easier for someone to make it up here before the plows came and allowed them to escape.

After grabbing his gun, he put on his boots and coat and stepped outside. His feet sank in the drifts, making it hard to move. He circled around several buildings and studied the road leading in, not seeing anything that indicated someone else had been in the camp. Satisfied, he returned to the manager's quarters.

Marielle was up and watching him from the window. The expression on her face, the raised eyebrows, communicated an unspoken question.

He hung his coat up. "I didn't see any evidence that anyone was out there."

She stared out the window. "It looks so calm." She pulled a strand of hair behind her ear. "At least the storm is over. Ian and I will be out of your hair soon. Can you help me dig my car out?"

"Actually, it could take all day for the county plows to make it up here. Maybe even not until tomorrow. Priority would be on the roads that have higher use. You'll just get stuck if you try to leave now."

Distressed, she shook her head and fiddled with the collar of her bathrobe. "Oh, I didn't realize."

Was she that anxious to get away from him?

She pulled a cell phone out of her bathrobe pocket.

"They don't work up here, remember?" he said.

She put the phone away. "I just thought maybe we could call and let the authorities know there are people stranded up here."

She acted like she couldn't tolerate spending much more time with him. "We just need to be patient and wait. I'll dig your car out so you can leave as soon as possible." He spoke softly, trying to hide the hurt her coldness toward him caused.

At the sound of small footsteps, they both turned. Ian stood at the open bedroom door.

"Hey, sleepyhead." Marielle rushed over to pick him up, talking in soothing tones and rubbing her nose against his.

The picture of the two of them together warmed his heart. Regardless of how Marielle felt about him, he could extend hospitality to both of them.

"Why don't I make the two of you some breakfast?" He wandered over to the kitchenette. "I have some shelf-stable milk left to make some pancakes. Got some canned apricots to go with that. Sorry, no meat or eggs."

"Food sounds good," she said.

When she tried to place Ian on one of the chairs, he shook his head and held on to the neckline of her pajama top. Ian remained in her arms as she took a chair at the table that seated four.

He opened another cupboard. "What does Ian like? I have some instant oatmeal."

"He'll eat the pancakes."

Graham turned on the grill and grabbed the pancake mix. After stirring the milk into the mix, he poured the batter out on the grill. He set plates and syrup on the table, then returned to the counter and waited for the pancakes to bubble so he could flip them.

"I see you've learned how to cook." There was a note of levity in her voice. When they were dating, they had a running joke about his various cooking disasters.

He managed a laugh but the reference to the past was like a stab to his gut. Now seeing her all these years later, he wondered if he'd made the right choice. Cesar's death had shaken him and made him wonder if he still wanted to be an agent. What would his life have been like if he'd stayed here and married her? Maybe they would both be in a better place.

When he'd left, he'd assumed she would meet someone new, marry him and find a greater happiness than Graham could ever give her. Graham placed the pancakes on a plate and put it on the table. "Sorry, no butter."

He opened the can of apricots and

poured them into a bowl. Marielle scooted an empty chair closer to her and encouraged Ian to sit in it. This time the boy complied.

Graham took the chair opposite Marielle. "You mind if I say grace?"

"Sure, that would be great."

Marielle bowed her head. Ian laced his chubby fingers together.

"Lord, we thank You for this meal. We pray for all those affected by the storm. Please bless this food to nourish our bodies."

"Amen." Marielle placed a pancake on Ian's plate along with some apricots. His head was barely above the table.

"Here." Graham jumped to his feet and retrieved a pillow from the love seat.

Marielle lifted Ian up so he could shove the pillow underneath the boy. "Better?" She brushed her fingers over the boy's cheek. Ian nodded and picked up a fork.

The kid had clearly been through trauma. Graham wanted more details but knew it would be wrong to ask while Ian was listening. He and Marielle would probably not have a chance to be alone. She'd made it clear she wanted to leave at the first opportunity. Seeing her stirred up old feelings. They would part ways as soon as possible. Though her anger was hard to take, he didn't blame her. A few hours together wasn't going to heal the wounds he'd caused.

After they finished, Graham gathered the plates and took them over to the sink. When he peered out the window, he saw smoke coming from the building where the washers and dryers were housed along with other supplies. The backup generator was also in there. Though the building was partly obscured by another cabin, he could see puffs of smoke rising into the air.

Graham ran toward the door. "Stay here. I've got to check something out." He raced toward the door, stepped into his boots and grabbed his coat.

She followed him. "What's going on?"

"Looks like there might be a fire." His first thought was that drifts on the roof might have blocked vents and caused some sort of combustion. He reached for his hat at the same time that his other hand was on the doorknob. The cold air hit him as he stepped outside.

As much as the deep snow would allow, he rushed toward the smoke. As he drew closer, he saw flames through an open window where the smoke had been escaping. He darted over to the cabin next to the one that was on fire where he grabbed a shovel propped against the door.

When he touched the doorknob, it was not hot. He pushed the door open. Though the room was filled with smoke, the fire was confined to a pile on the floor. He coughed and stepped outside, shoveling up a heap of snow and carrying it inside. He did this several more times. The fire persisted. He ran outside, coughing, to gather more snow on his shovel until he saw no more flames.

In the dim light, he studied the burned remains of the fire. He could just discern a fragment of an unburned sheet and a piece of a towel. He checked the shelf where the linens were kept in airtight containers. Several towels had fallen to the floor. He detected the faint scent of diesel fuel, which was used for the backup generator.

A terrible realization sank in. This fire was no accident. Someone had made a pile on the floor and poured fuel on it. His heart pounded as he ran outside back toward the manager's quarters just in time to see a man in a black-and-red coat reach for the doorknob. The man must have been hiding somewhere in the camp waiting for his chance to get at Marielle and Ian once he'd lured Graham away to deal with the fire.

Marielle and Ian were in danger. He tried to run as his boots sank down into the snow. He prayed he could get to them in time. He didn't want to think about what would happen if he didn't.

THREE

Marielle chose to focus her energy on Ian, trying not to think about what the fire meant. It could have been started by anything. Power lines could have gone down in the storm. Graham had searched the camp and not found any sign that anyone else was around. Still, the butterflies stirred in her stomach.

She'd taken Ian to the bathroom to wash his face when she heard the front door open. She breathed a sigh of relief. Graham must already be back. Crisis averted.

She stepped out of the bathroom with Ian toddling behind her. He held on to her bathrobe. "Hey—"

A muscular man with dark hair, not Graham, stood in the doorway. He smiled at her even as his voice held a note of menace. "Sorry about barging in. My car got stuck and I saw these buildings." His attention was drawn to the little boy behind her.

Her heart pounded as she reached a protective hand toward Ian. In his haste to take care of the fire, Graham had left the door unlocked. Marielle took a step back.

She felt a prickling at the back of her neck. "You were out driving in the deep snow all the way up here?" Her voice wavered, though she attempted to sound casual. Graham had said something about vacation rentals nearby. It could be the man was telling the truth. Still, she couldn't shake her feeling of unease. She continued the conversation to buy time.

He advanced toward her, his boots pounding on the hardwood floor. "I was hoping you could help me." The way the man lifted his chin and puffed out his chest struck her as aggressive. Plus, the man had just let himself in without knocking.

And he kept coming toward her.

Alarm bells went off as her heart rate skipped up a notch. She needed to get out of here with Ian fast. "I don't think that'll be possible. Why don't you wait outside until the manager gets back?"

"Oh, I think he's quite busy dealing with a fire." He turned back around, took a few steps and clicked the dead bolt on the door.

Fear raged through her even before he returned his attention to Marielle.

"Just hand the boy over to me."

So he *was* the man who had come after her in her home. She reached out for Ian, lifting him up and running to the bedroom. Heavy footsteps pounded behind her. She clicked the lock on the bedroom door. The man pounded on the door. "Let me in." The pounding grew more intense. He must be smashing against the door with his body.

Marielle slipped into a pair of boots she found at the foot of the bed and grabbed Graham's coat off the bedpost.

Ian let out a cry. She reached for his blanket and wrapped it around his shoulders, holding him close. "It's okay. I've got you." It wasn't just his physical safety she worried about. She'd do anything to keep him from experiencing more violence.

The assault on the door continued as she ran over to the window and flung it open. It was a short drop down. Ian lifted his head, round brown eyes watching her. This would be scary for him. She pressed her hand against his warm cheek. "We're going to have to go out this way. I'll let you down and then I'll come out right after you. Do you understand?"

Ian nodded.

"Thanks for being so brave."

A voice came from outside the window. "Hand him down to me." Graham. She thanked God he'd figured out what was going on.

The bedroom door had begun to splinter. She lifted Ian and helped him out feet first. Graham stepped back and held the boy while she put one leg through the window.

Her feet had just hit the snow when the door burst open and the man came to the window. Still holding Ian, Graham tried to navigate around the deeper drifts. She sought to step in the holes he'd made. The boots were too big for her, but at least they kept her feet warm.

A shot rang out behind them. The man had a gun.

Graham led her in a circuitous pattern through the camp around cabins. She thought she heard a noise behind her. Her heart pounded when she glanced over her shoulder fearing that a bullet would find its target. No sign of the other man.

She was not sure what Graham had in mind until he came to the back door of the main meeting house. He pushed it open and they stepped inside. "Get upstairs. There's a lost and found. You and Ian put on as many warm clothes as you can." He handed Ian over to her and pulled his gun.

Holding Ian, she headed past closed office doors, glancing into the main worship area before turning a corner where the staircase was. She had trod up these stairs hundreds of times and knew exactly where to find the lost and found boxes.

She ran by storage totes and shelves with books, binders and sheet music on them until she got to the lost and found boxes. This third story of the building had a slanted roof with windows at each end. Graham joined them, checking out each window and then positioning himself at the top of the stairs.

After putting Ian down, she sorted through the box, tossing aside swimming suits and shorts. "What is the plan here anyway?"

"There's a snowmobile in the garage."

She lifted up a child's coat. Too big for Ian but it would have to do. "But the roads are drifted over."

"I know, but the snowmobile will be more agile than a car." Graham stalked back toward the window. "He won't be able to keep up with us on foot."

She found a pair of canvas shoes and slipped them on Ian's feet over the socks he was already wearing. These would hardly keep him warm for long. Now she wished she'd had time to grab the go bag from her car.

She rooted through the box, retrieving a man's wool sock which she put over one of his feet. She wasn't sure about this plan. Without the proper equipment, they wouldn't stay warm for long on the snow-mobile.

She looked over at Graham who lingered at the window. "Do you see him?"

He turned halfway toward her and shook his head. "On the pristine snow, he'll be able to follow our footprints. It's just a matter of time before he figures out where we are. Did you find what you needed?"

Once again, she wrapped the blanket around Ian. "Not really." She held up a blue knitted cap which she placed on Ian's head. "But we'll make do."

He looked at the both of them. "You won't stay warm for long on a snowmobile. Maybe there is some more gear in the garage."

"Graham, I'm not sure if this is going to work. Will we even be able to get very far on the snowmobile?"

He studied her for a long moment. "I'm hoping we can get off the mountain. Maybe find some help." He rubbed his scruffy jaw. "But if we can't, we just need to get far enough away so he thinks we've left the camp, and then we can hike back in and hide until help comes."

So, they would be playing cat and mouse with a killer until the plows pushed through. There were no good options. "Whatever you think is best."

"Let's get going." With his gun drawn, he led them back down the stairs. He stepped out of the back door first, signaling that they needed to hang back. He gestured that the coast was clear. Once again, he led them around buildings that didn't provide a direct path to the garage but kept them mostly concealed. Both she and Graham had an advantage over the assailant in that they knew the layout of the camp.

While she held Ian, they both rested their backs against a cabin to catch their breath. Graham rushed to peek around the corner to make sure it was safe to keep going.

She caught movement in her peripheral vision. The man had just slipped behind a cabin not too far from where they were.

The assailant must have spotted them and sought to conceal himself for an ambush.

She sprinted toward Graham. "He's right behind us."

Even though Ian was small for his age, he'd grown heavy in her arms. But she had to keep carrying him. No way could he run and keep up. Plus, the canvas shoes he had on would get wet. She raced ahead as fast as she could while Graham took up the rear, still holding the gun and checking over his shoulder.

She reached the door leading into the garage and pushed it open. Nothing around here seemed to be locked. She supposed it made sense. Normally, there was very little risk of robbery or danger especially with a caretaker on the grounds. The garage had four bays filled with lawn equipment and tools. The snowmobile was on the opposite side of the building. The truck next to it must belong to Graham.

There was no time to put on the snowsuit she spotted, but she grabbed it and tossed it on the seat of the snowmobile. She hurried over with Ian, grabbing a child-size helmet for him as well as one for herself.

Graham stepped inside, twisting the knob to lock the door behind him. By the time he made it across the room, the doorknob was being shaken followed by pounding. Graham jumped on the front of the snowmobile without grabbing a helmet, but he'd picked up the garage door remote. In one swift motion he started the engine and opened the garage door.

A gunshot reverberated by the door. The attacker had shot the door open and stepped inside just as they zoomed out into the open, even before the garage door was completely up.

With Ian between them, she pressed close to Graham's back, praying that they would get away before another bullet hit its mark.

* * *

The echo of gunshots reached Graham's ears as he twisted the throttle of the snowmobile. Wind hit his face. His bare hands grew cold. There hadn't been time to put on his gloves. He veered away from a high drift and headed toward the road that led out of the camp. Though they traversed the smaller drifts and made it up the hill, it was obvious once they turned the corner that the snow was too deep even for a snowmobile to navigate through.

He chose a path closer to the tree line where the snow had not blown as much. He found an opening and drove into the trees, then killed the engine. Marielle scooted back so he could get off.

He stared down at the two people he was charged with protecting. Marielle had wrapped her arms around Ian, drawing his back close to her chest. The boy looked up at him, brown eyes filled with uncertainty.

He leaned down and brushed his knuckles over the boy's cheek, making a funny noise, which produced a faint smile on Ian's part.

He straightened up. "I'm going to hike out to a high spot ten minutes in one direction to see if there is any other road or way out or another dwelling close by. I'll come back in no more than twenty minutes. No way can that guy hike up here in that time and hopefully he'll think we escaped." Plus, they were hidden by the trees. His voice softened. "I know you two can't stay out here in the cold for long."

She nodded and rested her hand on Ian's head. "We'll be okay for a while."

As Graham stepped away, he heard her talking in a soothing tone to Ian.

He wasn't so sure about their situation. If they couldn't find a path of escape or some kind of help, the situation was dire. The temperature hung just above freezing at this time of day, but it would grow colder as the day wore on. As he'd speculated, their only choice would be to go back to the shelter of the camp, and the intruder might still be there.

Graham checked his watch before he stepped away from them. He pulled his gloves from his pockets and put them on. His boots sank down into the snow as he made his way to a high point. Once he reached the top of the hill, he had a view in three directions. A snow-covered hill blocked out much of Bridger, but he could see one of the buildings at the edge of the camp. He peered off in the other two directions, shielding his eyes from the sun glaring off the pristine white snow. No buildings, no foot tracks, no roads. He wasn't sure where those vacation homes had been built, but he saw no sign of them. They must be some distance away.

Following the depressions of his footsteps, he returned to where Marielle and Ian waited for him. Marielle had placed Ian inside of the adult-size snowsuit, and they both sat sideways on the snowmobile seat.

Her concern was for the child more so than herself. She had always been such a caretaker, and not only of other children. She had been perpetually adopting wounded animals too. It was a quality that he'd been drawn to.

She lifted her head when she saw him, a faint, hopeful smile gracing her soft features.

He stood several feet from the snowmobile, placing his hands on his hips and wondering how he was going to give her the bad news. Framed by the blue knitted hat Marielle had found for him, Ian's rosy cheeks and soft brown eyes were endearing. "Someone looks toasty warm."

She drew the boy into a sideways hug. "Yes." She pressed her nose close to his. "I figured he needed it more than me." She picked up one of the snowsuit arms and waved it around. "It's a little floppy on him."

"I can help you with that." He pulled a Swiss army knife from his pocket and proceeded to cut the excess fabric from the arms of the snowsuit. Ian watched him intently as he worked. Next he cut the pant legs, leaving them long enough so they covered Ian's feet.

"Much better." Marielle tossed the excess pant legs between some trees. "What did you find out on your walk?"

He stepped closer to the snowmobile, resting a hand on the windshield. "There's no way out where we won't risk being stranded in the snow and cold."

She lifted her chin to meet his gaze. Her mouth was drawn into a pensive line. "I guess we don't have a lot of choices."

He pointed in the direction of the camp. "I'm going to hike over and see if I can figure out what that man is up to. We can probably hide in one of the buildings at the edge of the camp if we can sneak in unnoticed."

She nodded.

What he didn't tell her about his plan was that if the man had chosen to remain at the camp, which would be the smart thing to do, Graham thought he might be able to take him into custody. He had to make sure, though, that Marielle and Ian wouldn't be in harm's way before he attempted something like that.

He needed to assess where in the camp the man was. Following the road that led back into the camp, he came to the place where the road looped around. He had a view of the buildings below as he perched at the top of the hill behind a drift. He could see the tracks that the snowmobile had made as well as footprints that followed at a short distance. Marielle's car had been dug out and brushed off. It may have been moved a few feet. The man had thought to follow them in the car but then realized the futility of trying to drive in the deep snow. He scanned the rest of the camp, not seeing the man anywhere.

Graham moved in for a better view of the whole area. Knowing that his dark clothes would be visible against the white snow, he remained low and moved quickly. Now he could see that smoke still curled out of the manager's quarters. Light glowed through the windows. Maybe the man was inside getting warmed up after trying to follow them in a car.

Graham returned back up the hill to where Marielle and Ian waited. Her face had grown red from the cold. She looked at him with expectation in her eyes. She'd found the pair of gloves he kept in the pocket of the coat she wore.

"I think he's inside the manager's head-quarters. Let's take the snowmobile and circle around to the back of the camp."

If the assailant remained inside, he wouldn't hear the snowmobile. That was a big if. He could be patrolling the area looking for them and Graham had just not been able to spot him. Walking on foot would exhaust them, though, and they'd get colder faster. They needed to utilize this snowmobile as much as they could.

Still holding Ian, Marielle rose to her feet, giving Graham room to climb onto the seat. He turned the key in the ignition. Marielle placed Ian behind Graham and helped him with his helmet, then put on her own helmet and climbed on too.

The plan was fraught with risk, but they couldn't stay outside for long. Though it got dark early, around five o'clock, they could not wait for the protection that the cover of darkness provided. They'd be too cold by then, and night would only cause the temperature to drop faster.

Graham chose a path where the snow was less deep. He could not begin to know what was going on in the attacker's mind. Maybe he knew they'd be forced to return to the camp and was just waiting for the opportunity to come after them.

Graham would do everything he could to make sure that didn't happen. He intended to arrest the assailant no matter what it took.

In any case, he felt like they were walking into the lion's den.

FOUR

Marielle hunkered down behind Graham's back, grateful that she was shielded from most of the wind and cold. Ian wiggled in his seat. At least he would stay warm in the makeshift snowsuit.

Lifting her head to peer over Graham's shoulder provided her only a partial view of where they were headed. Graham wove in a serpentine pattern, probably to avoid the deeper snow, and then headed closer to the trees.

When she glanced off to the side, a hill blocked her view of all but the outermost buildings of the camp. She shivered. Though Graham's coat reached almost to her knees, her thin pajama bottoms provided very little protection from the cold.

He veered away from the trees and headed downhill before stopping and switching off the engine. He turned his head slightly to talk to her. "This is as close as we should get. I don't want him to hear or see the snowmobile. Edge of the camp is just over that hill. We'll walk the rest of the way."

She got off the snowmobile, took off her helmet and looked around. They'd come down into a small valley that created a sort of bowl. The high roof of the three-story main building was visible, and smoke rose up from one of the other buildings, probably the manager's quarters.

He reached his hands toward her. "Here, let me carry Ian."

Exposure had made her even more fatigued, and she was grateful for the help. Ian didn't seem to mind the handover, nestling against Graham before they headed up the hill. She sank into the snow several times. At least Graham's tall oversized boots kept her feet dry. When they came to the top of the hill, she saw the camp down below. The white blanket of snow would not conceal them. If the attacker came outside and gazed in this direction, they'd be spotted. When she looked behind her, she could see their footprints in the otherwise untouched snow. If only the wind would blow and cover their tracks.

Her stomach tied in a knot. Though she realized they had no choice, it felt like they were walking toward danger. She said a silent prayer for God's protection.

Her face grew numb as they made their way downhill and came to the first building at the edge of the camp.

Snow had drifted over the door, making it impossible to get inside. After trying to open the door, Graham shook his head and pointed.

She tensed up.

They would have to go deeper into the camp, probably closer to where the attacker was. They trudged through the snow. When they came to the next building, Marielle opened the door while Graham held Ian. The door eased open. It appeared to be a storage shed for outdoor equipment. In the dim light, she could discern bicycles and kayaks. The building had no windows.

Once inside, Graham led them toward the back of the large shed. Still shivering, she settled onto the floor. Graham positioned Ian close to her. The boy turned his face toward her as if asking a question.

"We're just going to stay here for a while to warm up," she explained. They had no heat source and no food but at least they weren't outside. In response, Ian nodded. The snowsuit made swishing noises as he turned to look at Graham.

"We'll huddle together for warmth." Graham sat down next to Ian. "Why don't you and Ian get some sleep?"

That meant that Graham was going to try to stay awake and keep watch. She leaned her head back against the wall and closed her eyes. Now that they were out of the elements, her shivering subsided. Her arms and legs were heavy with fatigue, but her mind was alert.

After about twenty minutes, she heard Ian's gentle snores. Her mind relaxing a little, she nodded off. She woke up when Ian stirred beside her. Graham was gone. The door was shut, and the shed seemed even darker than before. She wasn't sure how long she'd slept.

Ian touched his mouth to indicate that he was hungry. "Me too, kiddo." She knew that even lack of a regular mealtime could set Ian back emotionally. She ached over what he was being put through, but she had little power to change it other than to comfort and reassure him.

She stared at the shut door. Maybe Graham had gone to find food. She imagined there would be canned goods or other mouse-proof items stored in the cafeteria, but that was in the main building in the center of camp, where they'd have a greater chance of encountering the attacker.

The door burst open. Marielle startled and Ian jerked as well.

It was completely dark outside. She'd slept a long time.

Graham rushed toward them. "He knows we're here. We need to keep moving."

Fear shot through her like an arrow. They were on the run again.

Graham's heart pounded as he reached out a hand to help Marielle to her feet. She turned to pick Ian up, and then Graham guided them toward the open door, stopping at the threshold to peer out.

Moments before, he'd seen the attacker. From where he was concealed, Graham had watched the other man discover his footprints and follow them. The footprints would lead around a couple of buildings before arriving at the shed where Ian and Marielle were hiding. That meant they had only minutes to get out of harm's way.

Adrenaline surged through him as he pulled his gun and glanced side to side. A flash of light shone several buildings over and disappeared. The man had acquired a flashlight and was getting closer.

Graham led the other two around the back of the shed through the darkness. They hurried to the shelter of the next building. Light flashed off to the side, and both he and Marielle pressed their backs against the outside wall of the building.

The goal was to move in the direction opposite from the man's path. Graham racked his brain for a semi-secure place for them to hide as they made their way to the next building. If he could find a safe place for Marielle and Ian, he might be able to go after the attacker and take him down. That would end the siege they were under, but he wasn't about to put them in the line of fire.

Marielle moved slower than Graham with Ian in her arms. He stepped behind her, searching for the beam of light that would indicate where their pursuer was but not seeing it. Maybe the attacker was having a harder time seeing the footprints that led to the back of the storage shed or he might have taken time to search the shed seeing that the footprints led inside the shed as well. Whatever the reason, the assailant had not yet come around to the back of the shed.

Graham hurried toward the main build-ing and opened a side door that led to the vestibule. The main building contained a sanctuary, the cafeteria and offices and third floor storage. Plenty of places to hide, plenty of entrances and exits.

Marielle collapsed on a bench.

"You stay here," he said. "I'm going to make it look like we kept running."

"Okay, if you think that's best." She was still trying to catch her breath.

He ran out the side door and toward the next building. Grabbing a branch to brush out his footprints, he backtracked a different way and created a second set of footprints alongside the ones he had just made. He found a set of footprints that indicated the pursuer had walked the camp earlier along with their own footprints from when they had initially escaped to the garage.

He was out of breath by the time he re-entered the vestibule. Marielle and Ian were barely visible in the darkness.

"I'm going upstairs to look out a window and see if I can find him."

"Ian and I are both starving. Can I take him to the cafeteria?"

He stared out the nearest window, which faced the direction they'd just come, seeing only darkness. The assailant must be searching each of the buildings, and that would slow him down. With so many footprints at the center of camp, it wouldn't be that easy to figure out where they'd gone. They had a little time. "I suppose that would be okay. No lights," said Graham. "I'll join you as soon as I can."

"I understand," she responded.

Graham went into the sanctuary and then took the side stairs that led to the second-floor offices. He peered out two windows but didn't see the telltale flashlight beam.

He watched and waited for a long moment. Only part of the manager's quarters was visible from here. Lights were on inside, but he couldn't make out anyone moving around. He'd hoped the man would just give up and return to the warmth of the manager's quarters, but it didn't seem likely.

He traversed the hallway to the other side of the building and stepped into another office. This window faced the direction where he'd created the misleading footprints. No flash of light there either. After running up the stairs, he checked the windows on the third floor, still seeing no sign of the other man. Wherever he was, he wasn't close to this building.

Graham hurried downstairs and stepped toward the back of the sanctuary and then through the door that led to the cafeteria. All the tables had been pushed against one wall and the chairs had been stacked.

He sped toward the kitchen. Just enough moonlight came in through one of the windows to let him see Marielle and Ian sitting on the floor. Both of them were munching on something.

Marielle half stood up. "Do we need to go?"

"No, I think we're okay for a little while." He sat down beside her and pressed his back against a cupboard. "He's not close."

"We found some breakfast bars and juice boxes in an airtight container. You want some?"

His stomach growled. He hadn't eaten since breakfast. "Sure."

She reached around Ian to pull the container toward her and dug into it. "Here." She touched the back of his hand in the dark and he turned it over. She placed something square in his palm, her fingers warm against his skin. Then she handed him a juice box and turned her attention to helping Ian with his juice.

She leaned toward the little boy, so her forehead was almost touching his. "Does that taste good?"

Ian made a positive sound and nodded his head. Marielle laughed.

It was the first sign of contentment he'd witnessed from the child.

Graham took a bite of the fruit-flavored breakfast bar. "Amazing what a full stomach will do for your mood."

"For sure," she said.

The brief moment of calm was interrupted by a noise from somewhere inside the building. Graham tensed. A door opening, maybe?

The kitchen had an exit that led directly outside. Graham bolted to his feet. "The garage is two buildings over. Go and find a hiding place. I'm going to see if I can take this guy down."

Marielle was already standing. "Oh, Graham. That's so risky."

"Do what I say. This will end if I catch him. Then we won't be running and hiding all night."

He was grateful that she didn't argue further with him. Instead, she picked Ian up. Graham opened the side door and checked that the coast was clear. The noise had come from the front of the building.

Marielle and Ian rushed down the steps and disappeared into the darkness. He said a prayer for their safety, pulled his gun and headed toward the sanctuary. Taking in a deep breath, he braced himself for a violent encounter.

FIVE

Marielle moved as fast as she could through the deep and drifted snow. Even in the darkness, she could see her breath as it came out in puffs. It was getting colder. Ian snuggled close to her chest. The silhouette of the garage came into view.

She kept trudging ahead, refusing to look back toward the main building. Tension knotted through her chest. She wasn't so sure about this plan. It was true that they would be safe if Graham was able to subdue the other man. But what if the assailant was able to overtake Graham? He would come looking for them, and she and Ian would be the next target.

The thought tumbled through her mind as she made her way past the building beside the garage. She couldn't put Ian at risk, but if Graham didn't have her help, they might all end up dead. There had to be something she could do to ensure that Graham was not harmed or killed.

She prayed that God would give her clarity.

Finally, she turned to check the main building, which was still completely dark. She could see the window of the sanctuary where Graham thought the noise had come from. Ian's hand clutched the collar of her coat. They had to press on.

She pushed open the door of the garage. There was enough moonlight streaming through the windows for her to see that there were plenty of places to hide.

Setting Ian down, she glanced around. After taking a few steps, she pushed aside a rolling toolbox to reveal a dark corner, a good hiding place. For two? Or could she leave Ian here to go help Graham? She had only seconds to decide.

Ian made a pleading noise, and she turned back toward him.

The little boy lifted his hands toward her, opening and closing them, as he gazed up at her. The face of innocence. She kneeled down and wrapped her arms around him, holding him close.

She had her answer. Her job was to protect this little boy and trust that Graham would succeed in his mission.

She touched his warm cheek with her fingers. "You and I are going to play a game. Do you understand?"

He nodded.

"We're going to hide—" she pointed in the corner "—and be very quiet until we hear that nice man's voice, Graham's voice."

Again, Ian nodded.

Marielle led him to the corner and both of them squeezed in. Hooking her feet under the toolbox, she rolled it toward her. Once it was within her grasp, she reached out and pulled it even closer. As the darkness engulfed them, she positioned herself with her knees close to her chest. Ian squeezed into the tight space beside her. She wrapped her arms around him.

The metal roof of the garage creaked in the wind. She closed her eyes and prayed.

Oh, God, give Graham strength, keep him safe. Protect all of us. You are our refuge and our fortress.

She would have to trust that God would help Graham as he entered into what might be a fight for his life…and a fight for hers and Ian's.

With his gun drawn, Graham entered the sanctuary through a side door and pressed against the wall.

Though his ears were tuned into his surroundings, he heard no additional noise. His own breaths seemed unusually loud in the room, which was otherwise heavy with silence.

As his eyes adjusted to the darkness, he could make out the rows of pews and the platform where the worship team and pastor stood. He surveyed every inch of the room, not seeing any movement. The gun felt heavy in his hand.

He'd been in gunfights before, but this was different. The lives of Marielle and Ian were at stake.

Barely breathing, he waited, listening and watching. The minutes ticked by, and he came to a decision. Deliberately, he made a noise by patting his hand against the wall. Then he took a few steps and ducked behind a pew. Graham heard no other sounds. If the attacker was still here, he would've reacted and moved toward the noise.

The man must have left the sanctuary. Was he still in this building as he searched for the people he meant to kill?

Graham edged back toward the door

he'd come through and out into the hallway, still not hearing or seeing any sign
of the other man. His feet padded softly
on the linoleum. Had the pursuer already
left the building?

A muffled noise reached his ears.

His heart pounded as he pressed against
the wall and took a few cautious steps
forward, trying to discern where the
noise had come from. Another similar
sound floated up the hallway. He moved a
little faster. It sounded like someone was
in the kitchen at the back of the cafeteria,
but the noise had been so faint, he could
only make an educated guess.

He hurried down the hallway and into
the cafeteria, then through the eating area
toward the kitchen. The attacker would
see the juice boxes and wrappers and
know that they had been there.

His heart pounded as he slipped through
the open door frame into the kitchen. But
before he was even across the threshold, a
heavy weight smashed against his shoul-

der. A second blow to his back caused him to lose his grip on his gun. He heard it hit the floor as he swung his fist and sought to land a blow against the other man in the dark.

Graham made contact with flesh, but he could not see clearly where the man was. He heard heavy breathing and lunged toward the sound, landing another blow. This time the man grunted in pain.

Motion flashed in his peripheral vision just as a fist connected with his jaw. The pain reverberated through his head, but he righted himself and fought back, punching several times. The other man slammed against a wall, and Graham dove toward the noise. His hand gripped the man's shirt. The assailant's heavy breathing surrounded him. The man grabbed his arm and twisted expertly, hitting a nerve that caused Graham to lose his grip.

Graham heard several footsteps as the attacker retreated. Silence fell once again.

No breathing, no movement. The attacker must have fled. Graham silently ran his fingers over the wall in search of the light switch. It was a risk, but he needed to find his gun.

The other man hadn't tried to shoot him, which made Graham think that either he hadn't had time to pull his gun or, hopefully, he was out of bullets.

Just as Graham flicked the switch, weight landed on his back, and he was thrown forward onto the floor.

He landed on his stomach, and the attacker pinned one arm at the shoulder and smashed Graham's head against the floor before he could react.

Sparkles traveled across his field of vision from the blows to his head and the sudden brightness after so long in the dark. Because his lower body was not restrained, he managed to turn enough so he could avoid another blow to his head. He could only see the other man in his peripheral vision as he fought to free his shoulder. He wrestled free and turned over, then rammed his fist into the attacker's solar plexus. The other man's face filled with rage as he wheezed. Graham had knocked the wind out of him.

Breathing heavily, Graham crawled on all fours until he reached the countertop, grabbing it to hoist himself to his feet. He was halfway to standing, scanning the bright room to assess the situation, when he saw the attacker reaching for something on the ground. Graham's gun. He couldn't get to it before the attacker did. He had to escape the line of fire.

He threw himself through the exit to the seating area a second before a bullet hit the door frame. The shot echoed in the empty space. He hurtled into the darkness outside the cafeteria and ran as quickly and quietly as he could. The other man's footsteps pounded behind him.

He'd taken Graham's gun. His own that he used earlier must be out of bullets or not operational.

Graham headed toward the sanctuary, plotting to use the side exit and ambush the attacker as he ran out after Graham. Maybe he could get his gun back. The sanctuary flooded with light. The attacker was already in the room. Graham ducked behind a pew, hoping he hadn't been was spotted.

The other man's footsteps padded over the carpet. "Come out, come out, wherever you are."

Graham clenched his teeth.

"What have you done with the boy?" The menace in the attacker's voice bounced off the walls of the sanctuary.

Graham crawled underneath the pew and then rolled to the next one. He could hear his pursuer walk past, working his way toward the outside door. Graham rolled and crawled under another pew, moving in the opposite direction.

When he came to the last pew, he stopped with his stomach pressed against the carpet. The footsteps had ceased. He heard no sound of a door opening and closing. The other man was not going outside to search. He must have figured out that Graham was still in the sanctuary.

"I know you're in here somewhere," said the attacker.

Graham held his breath and listened as the attacker opened and closed doors at the back of the room, checking the coat closet and storage areas. He needed to get out of here and fast. It was only a matter of seconds before the attacker searched the pews again and found him. He rolled out from under the last pew and kept crawling to stay out of sight. Footsteps plodded slowly up the rows on the other side of the pews.

Graham exploded to his feet. A shot shattered the silence around him as he raced back into the dark hallway.

He ran, pumping his arms and willing his feet to move faster. He sprinted past the cafeteria, seeking another escape route. The darkness would help keep him hidden. He pressed against a wall and moved slower.

He was nearly to the back of the building when he realized he no longer heard his pursuer.

Sweat trickled down his temple as he paused, leaning hard against a wall. He waited a few seconds, not hearing any evidence that the other man had followed him. Fear seized his throat as realization sank in.

The attacker must have gone looking for Marielle and Ian while Graham was occupied with his own escape. He knew that the woman and the boy were in the camp alone somewhere, vulnerable targets. Graham had to protect them.

He found a window, desperately searching for the other man. Outside, a light flickered by before disappearing into the building next door—next to the garage. Graham's worst fears were confirmed.

He raced toward the nearest door and

burst outside into the dark and cold. Light shone in the building next to the garage as the attacker searched. Graham slipped into the shadows provided by eaves of the main building to avoid being seen. He crouched as he ran past the building where the assailant was and headed toward the garage. He prayed that he could get to Marielle and Ian before the attacker did.

SIX

After she'd heard the second gunshot, Marielle had pushed the rolling toolbox out of the way and stood up with Ian in her arms. The boy had been wiggling from the moment they'd crouched in the corner.

She glanced around, searching for a better hiding place. Each gunshot had caused her to pray for Graham's safety. She had to believe that he was still okay. She knew she needed to stick with the plan despite her fears. Graham expected to find her in the garage so that was where she and Ian needed to be.

She set the boy down on the concrete floor and held his hand. "Let's see if we can find a hiding place with a little more room. How does that sound?"

Ian stuck two fingers in his mouth, tilted his head and nodded, staring at her with wide brown eyes. She glanced at a large plastic storage tote next to the empty spot where the snowmobile had been and then at the truck that must belong to Graham. As her gaze moved past the window, she thought she saw movement.

A moment later, Graham rushed through the door. Fear was written all over his face. He glanced in their direction for only a moment before nodding to the truck. "Get in, I'll get the garage door opener."

Scooping Ian up, she ran toward the driver's side of the truck. What was Graham's plan? The vehicle might be rugged, but it wouldn't get far on unplowed roads.

She sat Ian on the seat beside her and swept her gaze over the dash, grateful to find the key in the ignition. At the rumble of the garage door opening, she turned the key, and the truck engine hummed to life.

Graham yanked open the passenger side door and jumped into the cab just as she saw a bobbing light emerging from the building next to them. The attacker was no doubt drawn by the noise. She threw the truck into Drive before Graham had even closed the door and pressed the gas.

She saw the attacker just outside the nearest building, hindered by the deep snow. He held a gun. Her side of the truck was closest to him, and he only needed to get within range to make a fatal shot.

"He's got a gun," she barked, slipping down low behind the wheel as Graham bent his upper body over Ian, wrapping a protective arm around the boy. She sped up the road, or at least where she thought the road was, that led through the camp. A shot hit the front part of the truck.

She slammed the gas pedal to the floor. The buildings had provided enough shelter so that the snow wasn't as deep here as outside the camp. Still, it was only minutes before the truck slid to a stop, wheels spinning uselessly. She tried to reverse out of the rut the tires had created. The truck moved back a few inches and then the engine made a grinding noise.

Graham glanced over his shoulder. "No time. Get out," he yelled and gathered Ian into his arms.

Her heartbeat drummed in her ears as she jumped out of the truck, crouching low when she landed. She headed toward the front of the truck, which would provide a degree of cover. Graham was already several yards ahead of her as he held Ian close to his chest.

She followed as Graham sought cover behind the first building they came to.

Another gunshot echoed through the nighttime silence.

Graham stood with his back pressed against the building. "That's my gun, and I know he's going to run out of bullets soon. He has one, maybe two left. Go to the manager's quarters." He handed Ian to her, and the boy wrapped his arms around her shoulders. "I'm going to provide a diversion. There is a second gun underneath the plastic bag liner in the kitchen garbage."

She knew there was no time to protest the plan or express surprise that he'd apparently stashed weapons in the camp. She didn't want to be separated again, but she hurried to the backside of the next building as Graham ran out in the opposite direction.

She cringed when she heard yet another gunshot, momentarily paralyzed by the thought of what might have happened to Graham.

Trust Graham, stick with the plan.

Her heart pounded as she pushed herself toward the next building. No more gunshots reached her ears when she edged closer to the manager's quarters. Finding the back door unlocked, she moved up the stairs bent over from exertion and gasping for air but still holding Ian tightly.

Once inside, she put Ian on the floor and tried to catch her breath. They were in a little mudroom where some boots sat on the floor beside a tinderbox and a stack of wood. After locking the door, she ushered Ian into the living room.

Ian made a happy sound when he saw his stuffed giraffe on the love seat.

Marielle rushed around the house making sure the windows and doors were locked. When she peered out the windows, she saw no sign of either of the two men.

She pushed the love seat around so that it created a barrier between the windows by the front door and inside. She placed Ian on the floor by the love seat with his blanket and his giraffe.

"You stay here. Do you understand?"

The boy nodded and hugged the giraffe to his chest. Such a small thing made him feel more secure. She touched his cheek with her palm and looked into his eyes, searching.

"You're a good boy, Ian." She kissed his forehead.

He rose and fell into her arms.

She brushed the top of his head with a kiss, sat back on her legs and closed her eyes as she held Ian and rocked, praying silently.

Dear Lord, heal him from all he has been through, now and before with his parents, as if You pulled a curtain across his eyes and heart.

She rubbed his back and held him for a long moment before releasing him.

Marielle rose and moved to the kitchen. Taking a deep breath as she opened the cupboard, she lifted the trash liner and reached in for the gun. Her hand touched cold metal.

A small revolver. Six shots. Easy to shoot even for someone like her who was out of practice.

She put the gun in her coat pocket. When she peered in at Ian, he was pacing sucking his fingers and holding the giraffe. He needed a distraction. She searched several more cupboards for something that might serve as a toy for Ian. She brought him several small pots, a pie tin and a wooden spoon and showed him how to make music.

With Ian's light rhythmic tapping as background noise, she moved from room to room staring out each window for any sign of Graham or the other man. The gun felt heavy in her pocket. She brushed her fingers over the metal, feeling her throat grow tight. Could she shoot a person to save herself? To save Graham or Ian? Would it come to that?

She looked out into the darkness as a knot of tension formed at the back of her neck. The way Graham had laid out the plan had made it sound like he might risk his life to try to save hers and Ian's. The power of the sacrifice he was willing to make floored her. Why else tell her about the gun unless he thought she might have to defend herself?

The percussive boom of what he was pretty sure was the final bullet being fired surrounded Graham as he dove for the snow, praying he wouldn't be hit.

After a long moment, he raised his head and surveyed the buildings. With the gun rendered useless, he and the attacker were on equal footing. Unable to see much in the dark, he stared in the direction he thought the shot had come from. The man must have moved to the shelter of a nearby building...or maybe he'd opted to go after his primary target, Ian and Marielle. Graham's muscles tensed as he watched and waited.

Satisfied the man wasn't going to come after him, Graham rose to his feet and headed across the snow-drifted road to the side of the camp where the manager's quarters were. Aware that he might be watched, he didn't want to take a direct path back to Marielle and Ian.

He rushed around to the back of one building, keeping alert as he moved to the cover of the next. Worry settled in as more time passed without a sign of the attacker. The man couldn't have seen which way Marielle had gone with Ian, but if he was systematically checking each building, he would end up at the manager's quarters sooner or later.

Graham quickened his pace as the backside of the manger's quarters came into view. He reached the back door and found it locked. He'd knocked twice when a force like a brick wall crashed against him from the side.

The attacker was on top of him. Graham had only a moment to turn sideways so his face wasn't planted in the snow. Closed-fisted blows came fast and hard against his body.

Suddenly, the attacker angled away, lifting his weight from Graham's body as if reaching for something. Graham took the opportunity to sit up and grab the other man's ankle. The attacker fell, twisting away from Graham's grip and sitting up, holding something in his hands. Graham was still prone, and before he could react, the man attacked again from his seated position, pummeling Graham's torso and legs with the object. Pain vibrated through Graham's whole body, but he scooted away and got to his feet, the other man pushing to stand as well. Before the attacker was fully upright, Graham landed a series of blows to his face and shoulders, driving him into a defensive position. Graham reached for the object he held, fingers grazing wood. A thick piece of dropped firewood, perhaps? Something that could do serious damage.

The attacker spun free, still holding his makeshift weapon, and lunged. He struck Graham several times on the head, and then an explosive blow crushed against

Graham's chest. With the wind knocked out of him, the world seemed to whirl around him.

The attacker meant to kill him. When the man raised the wood again, Graham feinted and grabbed it from his hand.

The attacker swayed, clearly exhausted from the fight. Graham raised the piece of firewood himself, hoping to knock the other man to the ground. But his arm dropped. He too had been weakened by the fight. Dizzy and breathless, he bent at the waist.

He could feel himself losing consciousness even as he fought to stay upright.

God, help me.

The attacker saw the opportunity and dove toward him. Graham lifted the piece of firewood to defend himself but felt his strength draining.

A gunshot rang out from behind him. Graham watched the other man jerk at the sound. Another shot was fired, and the attacker scrambled away, running in the opposite direction until he faded into the darkness. Moments later, Marielle made her way along the side of the manager's quarters holding the revolver. She turned back toward Graham who had slumped to the ground.

"We need to get you inside."

He tried to push himself to his feet, but his knees buckled. Somehow, she got him up and into the mudroom. He must have blacked out for a moment. She had repositioned herself, so his arm was around her shoulder. She gripped his waist to support him.

His head bobbed and his vision went dark again. When he opened his eyes, he was slumped in the easy chair. Marielle had retreated to the kitchen. He heard running water.

Ian stared at him from the floor by the love seat. The boy looked afraid.

"It's going to be okay, little buddy." He tried to sound reassuring, but he tasted blood when he spoke.

Clutching his stuffed animal, Ian rose to his feet and moved toward Marielle as she returned from the kitchen.

She held a wet washcloth. "You're bleeding pretty bad." She leaned forward and touched his temple and then his mouth with the cloth. It felt warm against his skin.

Ian moved closer to Marielle and clung to her leg.

Graham's voice grew soft as he kept his eyes on the boy. "Is there some way we can make him feel less afraid."

Her free hand brushed over Ian's head and she let out a sigh. "Things could be going a lot better to help him heal, but we can't change what's happening."

She placed the washcloth on Graham's forehead. He winced. Ian moved toward him and patted his leg as if to offer comfort. The gesture touched Graham. Despite the pain he was in, he reached out and rubbed Ian's back. The boy leaned against the couch and stared up at him.

Graham rested his head against the back of the couch. "We have to be prepared. He knows we're in here. I'm sure he'll return."

"I know." She straightened up. The white washcloth had turned pink. She gazed down at him, then shook her head. "You're in pain. I'll get you some aspirin." She retreated again to the kitchen and returned with a couple of pills and a glass of water, which he gratefully accepted.

She scrutinized him, the lines of worry in her face deepening. "Graham, what do we do? You're in no condition to keep running."

She was right. Even when he tried to sit up straight, he felt dizzy. He needed to rest in order to recover. He had no idea what time it was, but morning couldn't be that far off. Would the plows show up by daylight?

She pulled the gun from her pocket and handed it to him. "There are four more bullets left. You're the one who uses a gun for a living."

"You handled the gun just fine. You saved my life out there." He took the gun and put it in the pocket of his coat. Right now, it didn't feel like he would even have the strength to lift it, let alone shoot accurately.

Their situation was not good.

Marielle sat down on the floor with Ian. She'd moved the love seat to create a barrier for her and Ian to hide behind. She picked up the wooden spoon and tapped out a rhythm on the pie tin, singing softly.

He recognized the melody. A song they used to sing right here at camp, but a world away from the dire situation they were in now. Life had been so clear-cut and innocent back then.

His eyelids grew heavy. He could feel himself fading. Marielle's sweet voice grew more distant as the blackness engulfed him.

He came to when Marielle shook his shoulder. "He's out there. I saw him."

Pain radiated through his body, but he had to find the strength to protect Marielle and Ian.

SEVEN

Worry lanced through Marielle's gut as she watched Graham try to push himself out of the chair, grimacing with pain. He managed to get to his feet, but he was still weak from the beating he'd taken. If he was to recover, he needed rest. She wasn't sure that was possible.

She pointed toward the front window. "I saw him through there. He went behind the sleeping cabin directly across from us."

He must have been prowling around this whole time, assessing the situation and waiting for the right moment to attack.

"I'm sure he's not going to stay there. He's probably trying to figure out a way to get at us, but he has to be smart about it. He knows we're armed. He doesn't know we only have four bullets." He looked directly at her. "You locked the back door?"

She nodded. "The place is as secure as it can be." She sat down on the floor beside Ian, pressing her back against the love seat and closing her eyes, hoping the silent prayer she said would quell the fear rising up in her.

Graham remained quiet for a few moments, and she opened her eyes again when he said thoughtfully, "He's taking his time to come at us. Do you think one of those shots you fired at him might have injured him?"

She shook her head. "I doubt it." She'd been shaking with terror when she'd pulled the trigger, so her aim was far from accurate. The gunfire had been enough to frighten the attacker away, no more.

Graham looked again toward the front window. "I wonder what he has in mind."

Marielle sat holding Ian while Graham moved through the house, crouching as he went past windows. Her heart pounded, and she struggled to take a deep breath. The attacker knew they had a gun and he didn't anymore. He wouldn't just break down the door and come directly at them.

Graham returned to his chair and sat down. He was sweating. The patrol had exhausted him. The bruises on his face had grown more distinct in the last hour.

She listened to the sound of his breathing and Ian nuzzled close to her and nodded off. She placed Ian on the love seat and covered him with his blanket.

Then she sat on the floor once more with her back resting against the love seat, her own eyelids growing heavy. She could feel herself fading again.

She'd been asleep a short time when the sound of shattering glass caused her to jerk awake. Graham was not in his chair.

More breaking glass, a window in the kitchen.

Her heart pounded as she took in a shallow breath.

She turned and touched Ian who was still asleep, but probably wouldn't be for much longer.

The taint of smoke reached her nose.

Marielle bolted to her feet. A burning rag had been thrown through the broken window. Another rag burned close to the front door. She raced to the kitchen for water, where she found Graham trying to stomp out a fire in there as well.

Cold wind blew through the shattered kitchen window.

Another window shattered somewhere in the house. Maybe the mudroom. The attacker was trying to smoke them out. Graham had already put a bucket beneath the kitchen faucet. Though it was only half-full, she grabbed it and rushed to the living room.

Ian was coughing. She was pouring the

water on the first fire when she noticed a third burning object had been tossed into the living room.

Smoke filled the room. Graham emerged from the bedroom carrying a wool blanket that he threw on the second fire just as another burning rag landed in the room.

Ian sat up and coughed.

"Get him to the bathroom. There are no windows in there."

She hurried across the floor and picked the child up. The hallway leading to the bathroom was filled with smoke. She sat Ian down on the closed toilet and grabbed a towel.

"I need you to put this under the door for me after I close it."

He let out a cry of protest and reached for her. She held him close as tears rimmed her eyes. "I know this is scary. I'll come back and check on you." She kissed his forehead then handed him the towel. "I have to help put out the fire."

He was clutching the towel in one hand

and his stuffed giraffe in the other when she closed the door.

The smoke had grown even thicker. She could hear Graham coughing in the living room. When she checked the mudroom, she found that one of the rags had landed in the box of kindling, where flames now rose.

She ran into the kitchen, grabbing several buckets from the cabinet underneath the sink. She put one bucket under the kitchen faucet and ran to the bathroom with the other. Ian was sitting on the toilet holding his toy and sucking his fingers when she stepped inside, turned on the bathtub faucet and placed a bucket underneath it.

She patted Ian's leg. "Thank you for being so good."

She closed the door behind her as she raced back to the kitchen where the bucket was nearly full. She could hear Graham fumbling around in the bedroom, probably trying to put out another fire in there as well.

She lifted the bucket and ran to the mudroom, where the flames had grown even higher. She saw that the fire was eating up stacked firewood and newspapers too. Her bucket of water did little to subdue the flames that licked at the wall.

Her face grew hot from the intensity of the burning. She ran back to the bathroom and picked up the now full bucket out of the bathtub. She grabbed a washcloth and dipped it in the water.

"Ian, put this over your mouth and close the door behind me. Put the towel back in place."

She was out the door before she had time to witness his reaction. In the mudroom, the flames had intensified. She poured the second bucket of water and turned to see Graham.

"You need to get in the bathroom with Ian. The attacker is trying to break down the front door. He probably thinks we've passed out from the smoke."

Sweat glistened on his forehead.

She grabbed his arm. "Are you sure?"

"It's the only way. Go take care of Ian." Graham pulled the gun from his waist-band.

She ran toward the bathroom through the hallway that was even more smoke filled. She found Ian sitting on the floor holding the washcloth over his mouth, his eyes watching her.

She touched the top of his head. "It's okay. I'm here."

After closing the door and putting the towel back in place, she wetted a wash-cloth for herself and then took him into her arms.

She could hear Graham coughing in the living room.

The burning smell seeped into the bath-room even with the barrier of the door and towel. They couldn't stay here much longer. The fire in the mudroom was going to get more and more out of control even if all the other fires had been put out. But if they ran outside, the attacker would be waiting for them.

The door flew open. Graham bent over and coughed before he could talk.

"Change of plans. There's too much smoke. We have to get out of here."

"Is he still trying to get in?" She rose, holding Ian.

"The noise has stopped. I saw him circle around the side of the house toward the back. He's probably assessing the damage the fires have done or trying to find another way in."

Graham reached for her, placing his hand on her back as he guided her down the hallway. The smoke stung her eyes.

"We'll go out the front door. The living room is the least smoky and I think he's still at the back of the house."

With Marielle in front holding Ian, they hurried through the living room. All of them were coughing as they reached the front door.

Her heart raged against her rib cage. She prayed they would find a hiding place before the attacker came around the side of the house and saw them escaping.

When he glanced over his shoulder, Graham caught a glimpse of the other man at the side of the house by the mud-room entrance, his back to them.

They had to hide before he saw them.

Adrenaline raged through his body. Despite his injuries, he felt a surge of energy.

He sped toward Marielle's car and swung the door open. "Get in the back. I'll keep watch."

Marielle and Ian crawled into the back seat and lay down as he closed the door silently. He slipped behind the back bumper just before the attacker reappeared around the side of the house. Hidden in shadows, Graham was fairly confident he couldn't be seen as he watched the man make his way to the front door. If he checked it, he'd find it unlocked now and realize they'd escaped. Graham pulled his gun and watched intently. Sure enough, the assailant opened the door and stepped inside. Smoke curled out from the back of the house. The man emerged a few seconds later glancing from side to side and coughing.

Graham ducked back behind the car, staying unseen but also losing sight of what the assailant was doing. He tuned his ears to his surroundings as the wind whipped around him. He held the gun close to his chest and pointed it at the sky while he listened.

He heard footsteps crunching in the snow, but they got softer as the seconds ticked by. When he scooted to the other side of the bumper and looked past it, he could just make out the backside of the other man as he stepped back into the main building.

The sky had already started to lighten. They would not have the cover of night to conceal them much longer.

It would take some time to search the main building and realize they weren't there. Now was their chance to find a more secure hiding place.

He rose and opened the car's back door. "Let's move."

Marielle sat up, inched to the edge of the seat and got out before reaching for Ian.

"Where is he?" Holding Ian, she drew the blanket over his head. She must've taken off the snowsuit at some point.

"Inside the main building." He surveyed the camp and made a decision.

Still gripping his gun, he directed Marielle and the boy in the opposite direction from the main building. She followed his lead through the camp and uphill to the sleeping quarters. He hurried them inside one of the larger cabins. The room was only slightly warmer than the chill outdoors. Eight sets of metal bunkbeds with no bedding or mattresses on them filled the room. Marielle had a vague memory from her time as a counselor here that the mattresses were stored where the mice couldn't get at them.

She slumped down on the floor away from the windows while Graham moved toward the window that provided a view of the camp below. It had grown even lighter out in the few short minutes it had taken them to get to the sleeping cabin. He spotted the assailant headed up the snow-drifted lane back toward the manager's quarters.

Graham ducked out of view. Still crouching, he approached the door they'd come through. There was no way to lock it.

Fortunately, there was no other door into the long, narrow cabin. Climbing through one of the windows would be too slow.

Marielle brushed a long strand of hair out of her eyes. "Now what do we do?"

He was fatigued and out of breath from the little bit of running they'd done to get here. Trying to play offense and go out to take the man into custody was out of the question now. He was too weak.

"Why don't you and Ian go over there by that wall away from the door?"

While Marielle shifted positions, he got up and peered out the window by the door. His throat went dry. The assailant was methodically searching each building working his way toward where they were hidden.

Assuming he moved in a straight line, he had three more buildings to look through. One of them was a small storage shed that would take no time at all.

Marielle settled with Ian against the wall opposite of where the door was. "Where's he at?"

Graham pulled a storage locker away from the end of one of the bunkbeds and sat down on it, facing the door with the gun in his hand.

He could not go after the other man and hope to take him down, but he could wait and be ready for him.

"He's coming this way," he said. "We have only a few minutes."

When the man came through the cabin door, Graham's plan was to shoot him.

EIGHT

Tension threaded through the space as Marielle wrapped an arm around Ian when they sat side by side on the floor. Her stomach was tied up in knots.

Graham spoke to her without taking his eyes off the door where his gun was aimed. "Why don't you and Ian get even farther away from the door? Back in that far corner on the opposite wall."

When the attacker came through that door, it was clear that Graham's intent was to shoot him. While she realized that Graham had no choice, Ian would witness more violence. Maybe he was hoping she could shield the little boy at least from seeing if not hearing what was about to happen if she was some distance from the door.

A chill set into her. Though she still wore Graham's boots, she'd slipped out of the coat when she was fighting the fire. She wrapped the blanket tighter around Ian.

"Are you cold?" Graham took his coat off, tossing it in her direction. "Put that on," he whispered before drawing his attention back to the door. "This will be over soon."

The intensity of his words made her heartbeat kick up a notch.

Ian stood beside her. He still clung to his giraffe while brushing hair out of his eyes. Not wanting to be spotted through the window, she crawled across the floor and reached for the coat. She rose to her knees and slipped into the coat which was still warm from Graham's body heat. "It seems like he should have gotten here by now." She lifted her chin but could not see anything through the window by the door from where she kneeled on the floor.

"Maybe he's moving through the buildings in a zigzag pattern instead of coming straight here. Checking more buildings that way." His arms, which had been straight holding the gun, bent slightly.

Marielle led Ian to the far side of the room and settled into a corner, wrapping the big coat around him after she pulled him into her lap. She could feel his torso expand and contract as she held him.

She peered at Graham through the labyrinth of the metal bunkbed frames. Ian slumped in her arms, resting but not asleep.

The seconds ticked by. More light streamed through the windows as the sun came up.

Graham let his hands relax. "Something's not right. He must be up to something." Staying low, he moved toward the window by the door to peer out. He shook his head and made his way toward another window.

Ian stirred in her lap and moaned softly. She made shushing noises, hoping it would calm him.

"I'm going to check outside," he said. "I won't go far."

She let out a fearful breath. "It's daylight." What if the assailant had figured out where they were and was waiting for Graham to step out?

"I have to assess what's going on. I'll be careful." He pulled the door open a few inches and stood watching for a long moment before stepping outside.

She steeled herself, waiting for the sound of bodies hitting the wall or gunshots. The silence settled around her. Even though he was weak from his injuries, Graham had a gun. He had the training to keep both of them safe. In a way, his leaving her all those years ago was now the thing that could save her and

Ian. Only God could have provided such perfect timing for her life.

She tried not to picture something bad happening to him.

Don't let your mind go there. You need to stay strong.

Ian wiggled in her arms. Eyes wide open, he lifted his head and stared at her and then patted her cheek. He must have picked up on her anxiety and wanted to comfort her.

"Sweet boy," she said. For someone so young, he seemed to be tuned in to the emotions of the people around him.

The door of the cabin creaked open, blown by the wind. Not surprising. The cabin was old and in need of repair. She stared at the door, deciding that the smart thing would be to stay put.

A single gunshot exploded outside. Her whole body jerked in response to the noise as her heart raged against her rib cage.

It didn't sound like the shot was right outside the door.

Ian sat up straight and twisted around. He slid off her lap and stared at the door swinging on its hinges. By the time she stood up, Marielle's mouth had gone dry. Her heartbeat thrummed in her ears.

Her attention remained on the open door. Ian pushed himself to his feet and reached for Marielle's hand. "Stay here. I'll be right back."

She ran to the nearest window that faced the direction the attacker had been moving as he made his way toward the cabin. The wind kicked up a flurry of snow, but she saw no sign of either Graham or the other man.

The door blew shut and open again, banging against the frame. The noise made her jump.

She ran back toward Ian and swept him up. This place felt really unsafe. But this cabin was where Graham expected to find them.

She'd taken two steps toward the door when she heard another gunshot.

Graham took aim and pulled the trigger just as the other man dove behind a pile of firewood by the main building. Once he'd spotted the attacker emerging from a building, Graham had pursued the man through camp. He'd used up two of his four remaining bullets.

His drive to keep Ian and Marielle safe masked his pain and exhaustion.

The wind had intensified, blowing snow tornadoes through the camp.

With his finger still across the trigger guard and his arms straight, he stared at the woodpile. The shot he'd taken must be lodged in a piece of firewood. "Come out with your hands up." The chase had left him out of breath and a little shaky but the notion that he was close to taking this man in energized him.

His hair ruffled in the breeze. His head and neck grew cold. There'd been no time to grab a hat, and he'd given Marielle his coat.

A faint mechanical noise reached his ears. When he glanced toward the main road, he saw snow spraying into the air. Relief spread through him. The snowplow was here and working its way down the road toward camp. They would be able to get out of here in less than half an hour. Hopefully, the snowplow driver would not been put in harm's way.

He intended to leave with the attacker in custody.

He drew his attention back to the woodpile as he stalked toward it then swung around to the back of it ready to shoot if necessary. The man was not crouching behind it. Tracks indicated that the man had dragged himself along the ground to stay out of view. Graham glanced at the corner of the long building just as the attacker disappeared behind it with a piece of firewood in his hand.

He was probably pressed against the

building waiting to ambush Graham and hit him with his new favorite weapon. The noise of the plow grew even louder as the driver made his way down the main road into the camp.

Up the hill, Marielle poked her head out of the cabin and was staring down at him. She turned slightly, noticing the plow. He gestured for her to go back into the building. He didn't want the attacker to know where she was in case this didn't go as planned.

Graham stalked toward the man's hiding place. With his back pressed against the outside wall, he moved a little closer to the back of the building where he assumed the man still was. He took a few more steps so he'd be close enough to get an accurate shot if the man ran out this way.

After several minutes, he realized the man was either still waiting or had run out in the other direction. He held his breath as he edged toward the corner of the building. Before turning the corner, he listened. Not hearing any indication that the man was there, he leaned out with his gun aimed, using the corner of the building to shield himself.

His breath hitched when he saw that the attacker was three buildings away. He was running along the back of the buildings and focused on fleeing, but he was still getting closer to Marielle and Ian's hiding spot. Had he seen her stick her head out of the building?

Graham had to get to them first. The plow had just reached the road that led through camp when Graham got to the front side of the buildings.

There was no time to wave the driver down and ask him to call the authorities when he got to the base of the mountain. Besides, he didn't want to risk the man becoming a target too. Maybe he would notice the burned portion of the manager's quarters and know something was amiss.

Graham headed up the hill to Marielle and Ian's cabin. He kept checking for the attacker as he moved but couldn't see the man anywhere. Though it looked like the fire was no longer burning in the manager's quarters, the blackened windows indicated that much damage had been done. Graham quickened his pace, praying that the attacker hadn't reached Marielle and Ian.

When he arrived at the cabin, the door was flung open. Fearing that Marielle was in a fight with the attacker, or worse, he gripped his gun and approached the window by the door in a crouch. His chest grew tight as he peered over the sill and scanned the interior. He saw no sign of the attacker—or of Marielle or the boy.

It took some mental effort to push away thoughts of the bad things that might've happened to them. Keeping his gun drawn, he stepped into the cabin. They were not inside. There was no blood on the floor, no overturned furniture, no indication that a struggle had taken place.

But she must've been afraid and taken shelter elsewhere. He looked through one of the small windows opposite the door. Tracks in the snow indicated where to search first.

He hurried to the next building, another sleeping cabin. The door burst open when he was a few steps from it. Marielle stood there. Flooded with relief, he stepped into the building and wrapped her in his arms. "I was afraid something bad had happened to you two."

He held her close. Her long brown hair smelled like burned wood but was soft to the touch when his hand brushed over it.

She pulled away and gazed up at him with wide brown eyes, the color of dark chocolate. "I was afraid he'd spotted me when I stuck my head outside the cabin. I knew we had to hide somewhere else."

They were standing so close that he felt her breath on his face when she spoke.

When he looked over her shoulder, he saw Ian standing close by, holding his blanket in one hand and his stuffed animal in the other. Something about seeing the little boy made his throat tight.

"I'm just glad you're both okay," he whispered.

She took a step back as her expression became sterner.

His show of emotion had made her uncomfortable. From the moment Marielle had shown up at his door, he had felt a responsibility to protect both of them. Maybe there were other feelings blossoming, but Marielle clearly didn't share them.

He cleared his throat and said, "The plows have gone through. We can get out of here now."

Graham stepped outside to check their surroundings. Down below, he saw the road through the camp had been plowed. When his gaze landed close to the manager's quarters, he saw that Marielle's four-wheel drive was no longer there. The attacker had chosen to escape in her car, probably fearing he might be stranded up here and caught now that the roads were clear. That explained why he hadn't come after them.

Marielle came to stand beside him. "The truck is stuck in the snow still. How are we going to get out of here?"

The plow had swerved around the truck as it plowed, creating a bank around it. Feeling a rising tension, he stared down at his truck still lodged in the deep snow.

The attacker had known which vehicle was usable, and which wasn't. He might have driven a short distance away and be looking down for the opportunity to come at them again knowing they didn't have a clear way to escape.

He prayed that they were not still trapped here, easy targets for their attacker.

NINE

Fighting off despair, Marielle looked at the tracks her missing four-wheel drive had left behind. "Maybe the snowmobile can get us out of here."

Graham stroked his beard before shaking his head. "That involves hiking beyond the edge of camp and a cold ride to the bottom of the mountain. Let's see if we can dig the truck out first."

She followed him down the hill. While Graham went to get another coat, she put Ian in the cab of the truck, turned on the heat and went to look for shovels in the garage.

By the time she'd found two shovels, Graham had returned. They worked together quickly to dig out the front tires, then shoveled out the bank the plow had made around the truck.

After about twenty minutes, she leaned on her shovel to catch her breath. Graham straightened and swiped his forehead with his gloved hand. He walked the length of the front bumper, staring at the base of the truck. "That should do it. You get behind the wheel and back it out, and I'll push from the front."

Marielle glanced toward the plowed road that led up and out of the camp. What was the attacker planning? He'd left them stranded here, but she didn't believe he'd given up so easily. Was he going to come back, or was he waiting for them somewhere on the road, knowing they could get out now?

She got into the cab and gave Ian's leg a pat before attempting to reverse out of the bank. The tires spun, the truck refusing to move. Shoulders slumping, she let up on the accelerator. Doing this was only getting them more stuck.

Graham stopped pushing and straightened to look through the windshield. She shook her head. He walked around to the driver's side window which she rolled down.

"I think there might be some kitty litter in the truck bed. After I spread that around the front tires, try putting it in Drive then Reverse, rocking back and forth to get out of the rut."

She nodded and rolled up the window. The truck bucked back and forth, finally getting out of the ruts the tires had created. Graham gave her the thumbs-up.

"All right." She let out a sigh of relief and smiled at Ian. "We did it."

Ian kicked his legs and hugged his giraffe tighter. Though it was faint, he smiled back at her. "It's good to have something go right, huh?" She ruffled his hair.

Graham came around to the driver's side, and she scooted over on the seat, lifting Ian into her lap and then setting him in the middle seat. While Graham climbed into the cab, she made sure Ian was buckled in. His car seat had been taken along with her car.

Graham continued to drive slowly, heading up the plowed road that would lead them back to civilization. "Once we get down the mountain and have cell service, we can call in a stolen car report. Highway patrol might be able to pick the guy up before he has a chance to ditch your car."

As they climbed up the mountain road, she craned her neck for one last look at the camp. "You'll have to tell Adrian about the damage to the manager's quarters."

"Yes, for sure." A note of sadness entered his voice. "It's hard to see that kind of destruction. This place has a lot of special memories for me."

"Me too." A flood of emotions stabbed at her heart. Remembering how good they'd been together made her sad for what they had lost. Like a movie reel playing, the memories spun through her mind. Swimming in the lake, walking the trails together, sitting around the campfire laughing with the other campers while Graham wrapped his arm around her.

"I'm sure the place is insured." He shook his head. "Still bothers me."

Was he remembering that this was where they'd met and fallen in love?

She gazed at his profile as he focused on the road and making the turn that would lead them back down the mountain. "Are you coming back up here to watch the place after you get Ian and me to town?" She still didn't know why he'd come back to Montana or why he hadn't gotten in touch with her when he did. Certainly, it wasn't just to be a wintertime caretaker. She pressed her lips together, feeling that stab of pain in her heart again. Graham still had a lot of explaining to do, but that didn't mean he would.

"Not sure of the plan at this point," he responded. "That man was after you two. While he's still at large, I need to make sure you're both safe, for starters."

"I appreciate that you want to help, and I'm so grateful for all you've done for us, but the local police will provide protection now for sure. I've been working with them from the start. We don't want to trouble you." She sounded cool, but her voice no longer held the tone of hostility she'd initially directed toward him. If the last couple of days had shown her anything, it was that Graham would do everything in his power to keep her and Ian alive. If she was honest, she would be a little sad that they were parting ways.

"It's no trouble," he said.

She studied him for a moment while his focus was on the road. Even though she felt herself softening toward him, the old feelings of hurt, confusion and anger were still there. When he'd hugged her with such affection back at the camp, she'd become afraid. The last thing she wanted to do was to open her heart to him so he could rip her world to pieces again. "You must have work that you need to do. Or are you on vacation while you're here in Montana?" The question was intended to probe for answers.

"Some bad things happened connected to my work." He glanced in her direction. "I came back up here to try to get my head in the right place." His words were clipped and filled with angst.

"I suppose the solitude of the camp is good for that."

"It always felt that way to me. I thought if I prayed and cross-country skied, that it would put me in a better place." He kept his eyes on the road.

"Did it?"

"Not really."

She wanted to know more, but the tone

of his voice indicated that this was not the time to press.

Graham slowed down as a car-sized lump covered in snow at the edge of the road came into view.

He veered the truck toward the shoulder as they passed by it. The wind had blown some of the snow off a sporty-looking hood.

"That must be his car," she said. "He made it this far up the mountain before he got stuck."

"We'll have to look into getting it towed. Chances are it's a rental or stolen, but it might provide evidence as to who he is."

Marielle stared at the car as they eased by. That meant he must've hiked the rest of the way into the camp in cold, windy conditions. Actions of a man who was determined to complete his mission and was also in extremely good shape. The memory of the attacker coming after her and Ian caused a chill to run down her spine. "He must be the man who…" She glanced meaningfully down at Ian, not wanting to mention Kristen's murder now. "Clearly he knows Ian can identify him."

Graham shook his head. "I'm not sure that makes sense. This guy had some skills and wasn't emotionally involved. And he didn't hide his face, which means we can identify him. I think a larger organization is at work here." He was speaking in lightly coded language too, shielding Ian.

"I think his intent was to make sure you and I were out of the picture and then take—" she nodded down at Ian instead of saying his name "—with him. He seemed more interested in getting him from us than doing anything permanent, at least at first." She drew her borrowed coat a little closer to her neck as if that would keep the icy terror from invading her awareness as she relived what had transpired the last couple of days.

"Yeah, he made that pretty obvious,

that we were collateral damage. Still, I think he might have been hired for this job. The guy had some skills for sure."

She hadn't thought of that possibility. If it was true that their attacker was simply a contract killer, then whoever killed Ian's mother wasn't just some addict who didn't want to pay his debt or was so messed up he'd lost control. And that made sense. After the killing, Ian's father had gone on the run rather than trying to stay with his boy. If the killer had resources, if he was part of a larger organization, as Graham said... Thinking about the home invasion and all that had transpired at the camp overwhelmed her.

"Course we won't know anything until we figure out who he is. I saw his face briefly," said Graham. "You did too, I assume?"

She nodded. Though it had been dark for much of the time, she did remember what he looked like. She'd seen him clearly when he'd first come into the manager's quarters. "I think if I saw a picture of him, I would recognize him."

"We'll give the description to the police. It'll make it that much harder for him to get at you two and easier to catch him."

"I hope that's true." She stared down at Ian who had fallen asleep. If the attacker was hired muscle, wouldn't the real killer just pay someone else to come after the boy once the attacker was caught? Would this ever end?

Graham got to the base of the mountain and turned onto the paved road that led into Clarksville. His gaze traveled from the road ahead to the rearview mirror several times.

She looked over her shoulder. "Do you think he's waiting for us along this road?"

"We have to consider every possibility," he said.

Though there was only a semitruck behind them, his hypervigilance made sense.

"Why don't you see if your cell phone works now? Call the police and let them know about your car. I have a feeling he'll ditch it at the first opportunity, so we need to be fast."

"I know who to call." She pulled her cell phone from her bathrobe pocket. After bringing up her contacts, she pressed the number for Detective Strickland, who was working on Ian's mother's murder investigation. He was her contact in the department. When he answered, she told him briefly what had happened and that they were on their way in for a fuller report. She wanted to talk about security for herself and Ian too. He promised to notify highway patrol to look for her stolen car. She gave him a description of the man who had tried to kill them. She realized her description was generic at best. Tall, muscular, dark hair.

"Sorry, I guess there was nothing overly distinct about him." She pressed the phone to her chest and spoke to Graham. "Do you have anything to add?"

He shook his head. "Nothing that stands out about his appearance. Only saw him in the daylight for a few seconds."

She talked into the phone. "Sorry the description is so vague."

The detective spoke up. "We might be able to produce a more precise description of him if we can get the two of you to look at the database of known criminals in the area or bring in a sketch artist."

"Okay. We'll get to the station as soon as we can. I just need to get changed and cleaned up. Ian and I could both use something to eat."

"As fast as you can," the detective agreed.

She thanked him and disconnected.

"Can we stop at a store? I need to get some different clothes." They were headed into town, not back to her house. She wondered if it was even safe to go home. Certainly not alone. Her world had been turned completely upside down.

"I get it, but I don't want to take too much of a chance with staying out in the open for long. Why don't we hit a drive-through so we can take it over to the police station and eat it there?"

She crossed her arms over her stomach. "I suppose you're right." Just a reminder that she could not take a deep breath until the man who was after Ian was taken in.

Graham rounded a curve and slowed down. "What have we here?"

Up ahead, the lights of several police cars flashed. Graham eased toward the line of stopped cars.

"Must be an accident," she said.

Graham brought his truck to a stop.

The line of cars was long enough that she could not see the accident.

"I don't like delays like this." His voice held a nervous edge as he glanced out the side windows.

She sat back in her seat, feeling the

tension sink back into her bones. "He wouldn't come after us with all the police so close by, would he?"

Picking up on her nervousness, Ian stiffened as well. She stroked his hair.

Graham's attention was focused on the patrol vehicles up ahead. "I don't know what he'll do. I just don't want to take any chances."

The line of cars began to roll forward. The car in front of them swerved a little. Graham shifted back into Drive and followed the other cars, keeping enough distance to prevent a collision if he did start to slide.

As they moved past the accident, she saw that neither of the cars involved was her stolen car. The attacker hadn't been behind them when they turned onto this road, and he wasn't in the line of cars ahead. "I don't see my car anywhere. Where do you think he went?"

Graham shrugged. "I don't think he'd just give up. Maybe he went ahead into town to wait by the police station since that's the most likely place we'd go."

They'd made it off the mountain, but that didn't mean they were at all safe. The relief she'd felt when Graham turned onto the paved road vaporized.

"Maybe it would be best if we just went directly to the police station. We'll figure out food later."

As long as that man was still out there, there was no safe place for them.

Graham drove past the accident. As the cars in front of him sped up, he did too but exercised a degree of caution. The roads were still icy, and it had begun to snow again. He was grateful for Marielle's suggestion that they go directly to the police station.

Though nothing bad had happened, sitting in traffic made him realize how vulnerable they still were. He vowed to work with the police to get the man into custody. He hoped that would end the danger for Marielle and Ian.

It seemed that Marielle preferred police protection over his anyway. There was still a chasm between them. He understood her anger over what had happened ten years ago. But still, it hurt to feel like she was pushing him away.

He glanced down at Ian. The boy's expression as he held his toy close to his cheek tugged at Graham's heart. To be so little and to have been through so much. Graham felt protective of him, just as he had felt protective of Cesar. It was just too easy to form attachments. Maybe he was no longer cut out for undercover work as he once was.

The snowfall intensified. Graham switched the wipers onto a higher speed. The road that led into town was winding. He pressed into a curve and focused his attention on his driving.

Once they got to the police station, he needed to get in touch with his handler.

He still didn't feel like he was ready to go back to work. He'd asked for a week off and only used four days of it.

If there was nothing pressing to deal with, perhaps he would return to the camp to help with repairs of the manager's quarters once he was sure Ian and Marielle had protection. Time spent being around and praying with Adrian might help him work through the loss of Cesar in a way that being alone had not.

Graham let up on the gas. Visibility was down to a few feet even with his headlights turned on. The truck swerved slightly.

Ian made a noise that sounded like a gasp that got stuck in his throat.

Marielle glanced through the windshield, then took the stuffed giraffe from Ian. Singing a children's song, she made the giraffe dance. Ian clapped his hands. Graham appreciated that she was trying to distract Ian from being scared about the hazardous road conditions.

While the windshield wipers worked at a furious pace, Graham gripped the wheel and leaned forward.

Marielle turned sideways in her seat. "That car behind us is really close."

Graham glanced in the rearview mirror, seeing only the headlights of the other vehicle made murky by the falling snow. "The guy must not be from around here. He doesn't understand about safe braking distance in hazardous conditions."

Though his attention was on the road in front of him, he could feel her gaze resting on him for a long moment.

"Yes, that must be it." Her voice came out in a monotone.

Neither of them wanted to say anything that would frighten Ian unnecessarily. But both of them were concerned about another assault.

Marielle's phone rang. She pressed the connect button. "Hello...yes...you found it already...where...thank you, Officer. We should be at the police station in fifteen minutes or so. It's kind of gnarly out here on the highway."

She pushed the disconnect button. "They found my car. Back up the road a ways. There's that café and bait shop that's right before the fishing access."

He had a vague memory of it. "Yeah."

"The owner reported his car stolen. They found my car up the road a piece, out of sight."

"Isn't that close to the camp road?"

"Yes, less than a mile," she said.

The man had not wasted any time in ditching Marielle's car.

When he glanced sideways, the other car had come up beside him. Passing in these conditions on a curving road was extremely risky. Graham lifted his foot off the gas.

Marielle let out a half scream that chilled him to the marrow. Ian stirred awake.

The other car was veering toward them.

Graham turned the wheel toward the

narrow shoulder of the road and sped up. The other car slammed into the bed of his truck with its front end.

Ian gasped.

Graham clenched his teeth. His body stiffened in response to the impact. Pain from his previous injuries intensified. Marielle drew a protective arm around Ian.

His truck fishtailed as Graham fought to regain control. He snaked along the road, praying that they would not meet oncoming traffic. In an effort to keep from wrecking, he lifted his foot from the gas. The erratic path the truck had been traveling in straightened out. He let out the breath he'd been holding.

Marielle peered over her shoulder. Terror lanced through her words. "He's getting closer."

He'd barely processed what she'd said when he heard and felt the jarring impact of metal crunching against metal. His teeth pressed together as his body was flung forward. The seat belt dug into his chest. His truck loomed toward the edge of the road as he sought to turn the wheel in the other direction.

A second collision to the back of the truck made it impossible to wrestle his vehicle under control. Snow swirled across the windshield while the wipers continued to work, creating a rhythmic and intense swishing noise at odds with the attack.

He pumped the brakes and tried to turn the wheel but to no avail. The tires left the road as they sailed through the air. The front of the truck impacted with a solid object.

He was flung forward and then back, pain from hitting the steering wheel roaring through him. The truck was too old to have airbags.

When the wipers stopped moving, the windshield filled with snow, blocking any view of the outside world.

He was breathless and light-headed. He turned to see if Marielle and Ian were okay, but his eyes would not focus. He saw blurred movement. Marielle wiggling in her seat.

His door opened suddenly. He was still restrained by his seat belt, so the attacker had the advantage, landing several blows to his head before Graham got in a single punch to the man's jaw. Black dots filled Graham's field of vision.

He heard the unbuckling of a seat belt and Marielle's protests coming from very far away as if she was speaking through thick fabric.

"Don't you hurt him," Marielle repeated over and over, her voice filled with panic and pain. She was close to his ear now even as he felt himself fading. "Graham, stay with me."

His world went black just as he heard the sound of glass being broken and Marielle screaming in protest.

TEN

The attacker smashed the window and reached in to unlock the passenger side door. She scooted across the seat to avoid the glass hitting her, though there was not much space with Ian between her and Graham. Her body shielded Ian.

"You can't have him." A maternal fierceness rose up in her.

The man grabbed Marielle by the collar. She shouted Graham's name, hoping to rouse him, but he was slumped over the steering wheel, blood dripping from his forehead. He did not move. Was he even still alive?

The attacker held on to her coat at the shoulders with both hands. When he sought to pull her out of the truck, she beat his arms.

The distressed and frightened noises that Ian made caused her to fight even harder. With her fingers spread, she clamped her palm over the man's face and pushed.

The man grabbed her neck and squeezed. In response, she clawed at him, wheezing for breath as she struggled to pry his hands off her, angling her body to try to break free in the restricted space of the truck cab.

The man's face was very close to hers. His eyes were filled with rage. The fear it struck in her only fueled her need to survive.

He gripped her coat at the shoulder with his free hand and jerked her out of the truck, lifting her slightly and tossing her on the ground, where she landed on her stomach. The snow was still coming down. Icy cold surrounded her face. She brushed away the snow from her eyes and cheeks, then turned toward the truck. The attacker was reaching in toward Ian.

She shook herself free of the terror that threatened to paralyze her. She had to save the little boy.

Marielle flipped around, grabbed the man's foot and pulled. His attention wavered, gaze flicking back down to her. She tried to scramble to her feet, but he pushed her back into the snow and lifted his boot. She drew her arms up toward her head and her knees toward her stomach to protect herself from the kick.

The impact never came.

She pulled her hands away from her face. The man was running toward his stolen car, which he'd parked in front of their wrecked truck. With some effort, Marielle pushed herself to her feet.

The attacker jumped into his car and sped off.

Swaying, she stared up the road in the opposite direction the attacker had fled. The flashing lights that filled her field of vision explained why the attacker had retreated. The police must have been headed back to town after dealing with the accident.

She stumbled toward the police car as the officer got out. A deputy she knew by sight but not by name came toward her through the snow.

He reached and held out a hand to steady her. "Ma'am, are you okay?"

"We need an ambulance." She pointed up the road. "A man ran us off the road. He drove away."

"I'll radio it in. What was the man who ran you off the road driving?"

Everything had happened so fast, she couldn't remember. "It was a dark color. The car that was just stolen from the café and bait shop up the road."

"Got it." The officer headed back to his patrol vehicle.

The sound of the officer talking on his radio became background noise as she rushed over to the truck. She peered through the open door where Ian had clicked himself out of his seat belt and was leaning against Graham, patting his shoulder. Graham's face still rested against the steering wheel.

The boy turned his head toward Marielle and spoke a single word. "Owweee."

Marielle let out a breath. Even through her terror, her heart warmed and a sense a joy filled her. It was the first word he'd spoken since she'd taken custody of him. "Yes. He's hurt."

At least, she hoped that was all that was wrong with Graham.

She ran around to Graham's side of the truck, where the door was still open. He did not stir at all when she spoke his name. Ian seemed to have formed an attachment to Graham. She prayed that he was all right.

She reached in, putting her palm on his cheek. His skin was warm to the touch, and the cut on his head did not look severe. It was the internal damage she was more concerned about. He'd sustained several intense blows to the head, both here and at the camp. She touched his neck to find a pulse, grateful when she felt the rhythmic push against her fingers. Ian stared up at her. His expression held a question as he sucked on two fingers.

"We'll take Graham to a doctor. He's going to be okay." She prayed that what she said was not an empty assurance.

Ian's face brightened.

"You like him, don't you?"

Ian nodded.

The officer came up beside her. "Ambulance should be here any minute."

"Can we ride with you to the hospital? We're supposed to go to the police station, but I need to make sure he's going to be okay." She nodded toward Graham.

"Why the police station?"

"This little boy witnessed a crime. We need protection. If you talk to Detective Strickland, he will fill you in," she said.

"Sure, we can do that, but why don't

you just fill me in right now? I'm Officer Zetler, by the way." He reached his hand toward her.

She shook his hand. "Marielle Coleman. This is Ian Roane."

"Roane, you say. I think I already know a little about this case." He looked at Ian. "I'm sure I can learn more when I read the police report."

She appreciated his sensitivity to not giving details in front of Ian. While they waited for the ambulance, she went to check on Graham.

She was grateful to hear the siren and see the flashing lights come into view.

Her stomach knotted as she watched the EMTs place Graham's still unconscious body on the stretcher, load him in the ambulance and close the door.

Ian held his arm out toward the ambulance, opening and closing his hand.

She snuggled him closer. "I know you're worried. I am too, baby."

The snow was still swirling down from

the sky as they drove behind the ambulance in Officer Zetler's patrol car.

They came to the edge of town.

As they rolled down Main Street toward the hospital, she found herself checking the rearview mirror and glancing around at the parked cars. She had a strong intuition that the attacker would try again to get to Ian, that he was waiting and watching for a moment of vulnerability. It was just a matter of time.

Graham woke up in a dimly lit hospital room. When he tried to sit up, his head was throbbing. The rest of his body ached. Despite the pain, he pushed himself up on his elbows. How much time had passed?

The curtains were drawn. No way to tell what time of day it was.

Bigger questions loomed in his mind. Had Marielle and Ian been injured too? Were they even still alive?

He tensed. The idea that he may have

lost them made his heart ache. Why had he not been ready when the attacker opened his truck door?

He reached for the call button, mind racing until, less than a minute later, he heard the padding of heavy-soled shoes. A nurse stepped into the room. She was a plump, fortysomething woman with brown hair, glasses and a kind smile.

She came around the side of his bed. "So good to see that you're awake, Mr. Flynn."

He touched his hand to his forehead, where he felt a bandage. "How long has it been?"

"It's nearly dinnertime."

He'd been out most of the day. "Was I given a sedative or something?"

"The doctor thought it would be best." She lifted a pitcher of water that rested on the rolling tray and poured some into a cup, which she handed to him.

The cool liquid soothed his parched throat as he drank. "That tastes good."

The nurse folded her hands over her stomach. "You must be getting hungry too."

His stomach was growling but he had more important things on his mind. "When can I get out of here?"

"The good news is that you don't have any broken bones. You're just very bruised and cut up and you have a concussion. Once the doctor gives the okay, you'll be free to go."

He handed her the cup. Trying to get a deep breath hurt his chest. He must have bruised it when he slammed into the steering wheel. The memory of the collision and the attack made him shudder.

He had to ask the question he'd been dreading. He had to know. "There was a woman and child with me in the truck."

The nurse patted his arm just above the elbow. "They're here. They've been waiting for you to wake up. Would you like to see them?"

"You mean they're okay?" He finally

felt like he could fill his lungs with air as relief and joy spread through him.

"Yes, they're both just fine," said the nurse. "The doctor already checked them out."

"Yes, I'd like to see them." Marielle had cared about him enough to stay around. It was a risk for her not to go directly into police protection.

"I believe they went downstairs to the cafeteria," said the nurse. "But I'll let them know when they come back. They both were quite worried about you."

A sense of panic made him try to sit up again. "They shouldn't be wandering through this hospital alone."

She straightened his pillow, so it was propped against the wall and then helped him into a sitting position. "No need to worry. A police officer has been with them this whole time."

He relaxed a little, but his heart was still pounding. Though he was grateful that Marielle had gotten an officer to stay with her and Ian, they would remain in danger as long as the man who had come after them was at large. He had to do what he could to make sure he was brought to justice.

"Can I have my phone? It should be in the zippered pocket of my coat." He needed to call his handler to see if he could stay and help Marielle and Ian…if she would let him.

"Sure, I'll bring it to you. But I think we better also get some food in you. I'll see what the food services can bring up for you."

The nurse retrieved his phone for him and left the room, and he was relieved to see the battery still had a little charge.

His thumb hovered over his handler's number, and for the first time in hours, he thought of Cesar. The young man's death would continue to haunt him. But the time for retreat and refuge was over. He wasn't about to have someone else die on his watch.

He called his handler. Bruce picked up on the second ring.

"Agent Flynn, I was wondering when you were going to check in. We had an interesting development in your neck of the woods."

"Really?" He tried to sit up straighter, but his head throbbed.

"Do you remember that truck we were going to follow to try to identify key players in drug transport?"

"Yes, the one Cesar told me about." Though the truck was scheduled to haul produce from Mexico to the States, Cesar had learned that it would have drugs hidden in it too.

"It left Mexico January thirteenth and seems to have ended up not too far from where you are. We found the truck, empty of course, but K-9s detected drug residue. Are you in a better head space and ready to get back to work?"

What a loaded question. He wondered how much he even needed to share about what had happened. The man at the camp was after Ian and needed him and Marielle out of the way, but the murder of Ian's mother was a case for the local police. "I'm as good as I'm ever going to be. It's a long story, but I had some injuries that put me in the hospital."

"You going to be all right?"

"I'm fine." He wanted to focus on the case. "So you found the truck but nothing on the driver?"

"Actually, we found out quite a bit. We have a name for our truck driver. But we don't think it's a regular cartel guy. Our techs have been combing through surveillance footage at the border trying to figure out when this guy crossed down into Mexico to get that truck. We got a positive ID on a car with a Montana plate registered to a Charlie Roane."

Marielle and Ian stepped into Graham's room, a police officer hovered just outside the door. Ian's eyes lit up when he saw Graham, and Graham waved his free hand at the child. Marielle was wearing clothes that looked like something she'd gotten in the hospital gift shop: leggings and long T-shirt with a Christmas image on it. She still wore his oversized coat. They exchanged smiles before Graham turned his attention back to the phone call.

"The car was found in Mexico?" he prompted Bruce.

"Yeah. The car is registered for Lane County in a town not too far from where you grew up, not reported as stolen so we can be reasonably sure it's Charlie Roane we're looking for. We found the car abandoned in Mexico. Mexican authorities have agreed to turn it over. Our forensics guys will go through it, but I don't think it's our strongest lead."

Graham shifted in his bed which caused pain to slice through his head. "So, the million-dollar question is: Was Charlie Roane working for the cartel or did he steal the shipment from the cartel?"

Marielle startled and gripped the bed railing, her expression darkening from the welcoming smile she'd worn a few seconds earlier. Ian drew his brows together and moved toward Marielle, grabbing the hem of her coat. He wondered what had caused the sudden mood change.

Bruce said, "We need to track down Charlie. Also, we'll probably need the support of local law enforcement. They've been briefed on the case and one of the officers already went to Charlie's last known residence. Of course, he'd cleared out."

There was more he wanted to talk to Bruce about, but he sensed that Marielle was upset about something. "Thanks for doing that. I'll call you back in a bit." He disconnected and looked up at her. "Everything okay?"

"What's going on with the man named Charlie Roane?"

Ian jerked his head up, his focus intently on Marielle.

"He's an important piece in an investigation I'm working on. Why?"

Marielle's face had drained of color. She scooted Ian toward the door. "Ian, why don't you go talk to the nice policeman?" She said something to the officer, turned and closed the door. "I didn't want him to hear this." She stepped closer to the front of Graham's bed. "Charlie Roane is the brother of Ian's missing father, David."

Graham was trying to process what she was saying. "David is the man who disappeared after Ian's mother was killed?"

She nodded. "The police don't think he killed Kristen, but they don't know why he's gone into hiding."

Graham spoke in a low voice. "Maybe he feared for his life." That would be the case if the cartel was somehow involved. He rubbed his beard, wondering what the connection might be. Maybe it was coincidence. Two brothers involved in separate crimes. "What was the exact date of Kristen's murder?"

"January sixteenth," she said.

The man they now knew was Charlie had been seen leaving Mexico in the truck on January thirteenth. It was approximately forty hours of driving to get from the middle of Mexico to southwest Montana.

Charlie had been out of state when Kristen was killed.

Marielle tugged on the open zipper of her coat, saying the words that he had been thinking. "What if these two cases are connected?"

"They could be." If the cases were linked, the implications were frightening. "If that's so, it would confirm that Kristen wasn't killed by some addict who thought he'd been slighted. This whole thing could link back to the cartel. The drugs hidden in that truck were most likely theirs. We don't know if Charlie was working for them or someone else.

Maybe he was their regular pickup guy for northwest deliveries. We need to find out more about him."

"You think Kristen's death somehow connects to the cartels?" Her voice cracked.

He saw the fear in her face. He couldn't lie to her, even though the words caused a tightening in his gut. "It's a high probability at this point, which means we're dealing with some very dangerous people."

ELEVEN

Marielle drew Graham's open coat tighter around her body and crossed her arms, fighting off a chill that had nothing to do with the temperature of the room.

Her mind reeled. "That makes it all the more likely that the man who came after Ian and me was a hired killer."

"True." He reached out to rub her arm, which comforted her a little. "The only way we will know for sure will be for us to figure out who that man was and catch him."

She took a step back, shaking her head. "This is all too much."

Graham was using the word *we* a lot. So much had changed since the shock of seeing him only two nights ago at the camp. She appreciated that he wanted to protect her, and Ian seemed to have grown attached to him, but the wounds his departure had caused and the pain from the destruction of all her hopes and dreams were far from healed. Now that the immediate threat had receded, it was impossible to keep the hurt at bay. It would only worsen if she spent more time around him.

The realization of who was behind Kristen's death made her thoughts turn to Ian. "I have something encouraging to tell you. Ian spoke for the first time since the murder. He expressed concern about you when you were unconscious in the truck."

He sat up a little straighter. "Really? That's great."

"He…cares about you. He hasn't spoken a word since, but it's a good sign."

"I think it's wonderful." He shook his head. "Poor little guy. He deserves a chance at overcoming all that he has seen in his short life."

Graham had connected with the child as much as Ian was drawn toward Graham. She stared at him for a moment, relishing the warmth she saw in his eyes before looking toward the door.

Though she was still trying to process what all this meant, it felt like the conversation was over for now.

"I'll go check on him," she said instead. A sense of urgency to see Ian compelled her out of the room. He sat on a chair in the hallway with Officer Zetler beside him. He was eating a bag of chips that they must have gotten from a vending machine. Orange dust covered the area around his mouth.

She held her arms open to him. The boy slipped off the chair and ran to her. She lifted him and stood up, his smooth cheek brushing against hers as he shifted the bag of chips.

"I'll stay right here," said the officer.

She set Ian back down inside Graham's room, and the boy walked over to Graham, who was propped up in the bed. He pulled a chip out of his bag and held it up toward Graham.

"For me?" Graham reached down and took the chip. "Thanks, buddy."

A bond had definitely formed between the two of them. She wasn't sure if that was a good thing.

Ian handed Graham another chip.

Graham crunched on it loudly. "Yum yum. Mmmm good."

Ian lifted his chin and giggled.

It warmed her heart to see the boy's face so filled with life. At the same time, it made her afraid. She thought of how Graham had left so abruptly ten years ago. He'd claimed it had been for his new career, or had that been an excuse to get away from her? Did commitment scare him? Would he just disappear again, and this time hurt a little boy too? So many unanswered questions.

The nurse stood in the open door holding a tray. "Suppertime."

Marielle took a step back from the bed and from the feelings and thoughts that threatened to overwhelm her.

While the nurse set up the meal on Graham's rolling table tray, Marielle pulled a chair closer to Graham's bed and sat down. Ian wandered over to her, and she pulled him onto her lap.

After the nurse left, Graham took a few bites of his meat loaf and potatoes. Ian munched on his last chip and then held the empty bag up for Marielle to see.

"Are you still hungry?"

Graham smiled at Ian. "Thanks for sharing with me. You can have my cookie if you like." He held the cookie out.

Ian slid out of Marielle's lap and walked over to get the cookie, swaying his body back and forth in delight as he nibbled. Was it a good thing he was bonding to Graham? Her primary job was to protect

Ian not just from physical harm but emotional hurt as well.

"So are you working on the case that Charlie Roane is connected to?" She needed to know how soon he would exit from their lives.

He scooted food around on his plate with his fork, making a scraping noise. "Yes, I think so. I'm here. I know this part of the state pretty well."

Time to ask the question she was most concerned about. "After your case is wrapped up, will you be leaving Montana again? That is the nature of your work, right?"

"Yes, my job takes me all over North and South America," he said.

She laced her fingers together. "Do you enjoy what you do?"

Ian had come over and was standing by her chair while he ate the last bites of his cookie.

"I like that it feels like I make a difference." Graham took a bite of food and then rested his head against the propped-up pillows. "I used to feel that way, anyhow. I loved my job, but some things have changed so I don't know anymore."

"You mentioned something bad happened?"

He put his fork down and stared off into space. "A teenage boy I cared about who was helping me with a case was killed." His voice had become heavy with emotion. "His name was Cesar. Just a kid."

She shifted in her chair, not sure what to say. "I'm sorry. That sounds hard." When she looked at Ian, he was occupied feeding pretend bites of cookie to his giraffe. She was glad he wasn't tuned into their conversation.

"It's never okay to have someone die on my watch." He shook his head. "It's not right, and I can't fix it."

A heavy silence settled into the room. Graham was dealing with a great deal of pain and confusion connected with his job that she could not begin to fathom.

She rose and reached out to put her hand on his.

Ian had finished his cookie and was dancing from one foot to the other. His antics broke the intensity of the moment.

"He has to go to the bathroom." She stood up and took Ian's hand. "I'll be right back."

With Ian walking beside her, she hurried out the door and by Officer Zetler. "Potty run," she explained as they passed.

Officer Zetler nodded and followed them down the hall. She ushered Ian into the bathroom and opened a stall for him. "Do you need my help?"

Ian shook his head. She waited in the bathroom by the sinks until he was done and then lifted him up to the sink to help him wash his hands. She had just pulled out a paper towel for him when a shrill noise filled the air.

The fire alarm. Her heart raced.

Ian put his hands over his ears. His features crinkled up in agony and he bent over.

She swept him up into her arms. "It's okay." Her voice was barely audible over the auditory assault.

She entered the hallway, not seeing Officer Zetler anywhere. Several people rushed past. Her heart pounded as she caught the attention of a nurse. "Where is the nearest exit?"

The nurse pointed down an adjoining hallway as she ran by. "I have to go. We need to get the patients out."

Marielle moved to go up the hall. "I need to help my friend."

The nurse squeezed her arm. "No, you need to get out now. We'll take care of him."

She ran toward where the nurse had pointed.

Perhaps Officer Zetler had gone to help get the less mobile patients outside.

Still holding Ian in one arm, she pushed open the exit door.

She came out into a parking lot at the back of the hospital where a large group of people were milling around. Many of them were staring at the hospital, probably trying to figure out where the fire was. Some were dressed in medical uniforms and others must have been in the waiting room or were patients with minor injuries.

No flames furled out of any windows. She hadn't smelled smoke while inside. If there was a fire, it must be deep within the building.

Now that they were outside, the intensity of the alarm had lessened, but Ian still had his hands against his ears.

She pressed her face close to his as she walked away from the building. "It's not as loud now. You can put your hands down."

Ian gingerly pulled his hands away. She stood off from the group of people who had escaped to this parking lot. Several more people came out of the exit and joined the crowd.

A short, bald man with his arm in a sling came up to her. "Excuse me, are you Marielle?"

She blinked in surprise. "Yes. How did you know?"

"A man named Graham described you and the boy. He's not very mobile. He asked me to find you and let you know that he's looking for you."

"Oh, he must be worried about us," she said. If only she'd been in the room with him when the alarm had gone off. He would know she got out safe.

"He said you could meet him by the pocket park with the horse sculpture."

She was familiar enough with the hospital that she knew the area the man was talking about.

The hospital was shaped like an H with somewhat crooked arms, which created lots of nooks and crannies. The park was in one of those nooks. Carrying Ian, she hurried around the hospital grounds, compelled by the need to assure Graham that she and Ian were okay. She encountered another cluster of people outside an emergency exit. They too were looking at the hospital, where there still was no sign or smell of a fire.

She slowed down as she turned the last corner and neared the little park. Sheltered on three sides by the strangely shaped hospital walls, the park was quiet and peaceful, tucked out of sight of the crowd she'd just walked through.

She took a few more slow steps, and the horse sculpture at the edge of the park came into view. No people milled around the area. This section of the hospital was bordered by a grove of trees without connection to a parking lot. The wind made the bare branches creak.

The park appeared unoccupied.

Though she saw nothing suspicious, her

heart beat a little faster. She had the sense that someone was close by, watching her.

She swallowed to get rid of the lump in her throat. "Graham?" Ian wiggled in her hold as she took another step toward the park. An empty bench came into view.

Something didn't feel right. Still holding Ian, she turned to go back to the crowd by the emergency exit.

She heard footsteps behind her. She looked over her shoulder and screamed. The attacker from the camp was running toward them.

She let out another scream, knowing she could not outrun him with Ian in her arms and praying someone would hear and come to help them.

The attacker caught up with her. He grabbed the hood of her coat and then tightened his hand around her upper arm, spinning her around as he sought to wrench Ian from her.

She screamed again.

People came running from several different directions. The attacker glanced around, assessing, then let go of Marielle and fled toward the trees.

Graham, dressed in a hospital gown and coat, burst out of the crowd and chased after the man. Officer Zetler was behind him.

Out of breath and shaking, she held Ian close.

The nurse who had been in Graham's room came toward her, wrapping her arm around Marielle's shoulder. "I saw what happened. That must've been very frightening." She ushered Marielle toward a bench.

The bald man with his arm in a sling had set her up. Maybe the attacker had given him money or just told a lie and said he was Graham.

Marielle's heart was still pounding as she sat down. Ian clung to her neck. She kissed the top of his blond head and hugged him tight. "I know that was scary for you."

She wanted to say that it would never happen again, that she would keep him safe no matter what. With every ounce of strength she had, she intended to protect him, but it was clear that whoever they were up against were determined to hurt Ian.

A few moments later, an administrator announced, "We can go back inside. Turns out there was no fire."

The kind nurse supported Marielle's elbow as she rose from the bench. "Do you think someone pulled it to raise a false alarm?" Marielle asked.

"Looks that way," said the nurse as she led them back toward the hospital.

The attacker must have done it to get Marielle outside and vulnerable where he could get at Ian.

Before entering the hospital, she gazed in the direction that Graham and the officer had gone, praying that they would capture the attacker.

* * *

As he ran, Graham struggled for air. His side hurt from the exertion. His injuries had weakened him. Determined to not let this man get away, he willed himself to keep going.

The attacker sprinted into the trees by the pocket park and Graham followed, with the officer close behind him. The row of trees bordered an empty parking lot by a disused building. Snow covered the sidewalks and the windows were boarded up.

Both men stopped abruptly, not seeing any sign of the attacker. Graham did not hear retreating footsteps. The guy had to be hiding somewhere. He surveyed the area until his eye caught movement.

"There." Graham pointed to a hedge on the other side of the parking lot.

Graham sprinted across the concrete while the officer stopped to call for backup on his radio.

When Graham got to the hedge, he

spotted the man crouching behind it to conceal himself as he moved along it.

The attacker glanced over his shoulder. He straightened at the sight of Graham and broke into a run again, bursting across the street and running toward a residential area.

Pumping his legs, Graham fought to fill his lungs with air and get beyond the pain and weakness that slowed him down. He closed the distance between himself and the other man.

The attacker darted behind a house. Graham followed, coming out into a back lane where he saw no sign of the man he was chasing.

Officer Zetler caught up with Graham. He spoke between breaths. "Backup is on the way."

"He's around here somewhere." Graham glanced up and down the lane. The attacker could have gone in one of two directions—deeper into the subdivision or out toward the street. "You go that way." Graham pointed toward the houses before choosing the second option for himself.

He ran through the edge of the subdivision and out onto the street. Across from him were houses that were under construction. Some had been framed, others were only concrete slabs. Everywhere there were stacks of construction materials and piles of dirt along with heavy equipment. There were no construction workers around. Of course, it was Sunday. He'd lost track of the days.

He caught movement in his peripheral vision by a stack of wooden pallets. Graham ducked behind a backhoe that was close to the pallets. He saw the attacker from behind as he peered out, clearly looking for Graham.

His gun had been taken off him, he assumed when he was admitted to the hospital, but he still had the element of surprise on his side if he acted fast.

Graham ducked under the arm of the backhoe and rushed toward the man.

The man turned just as Graham was about to jump him. Graham stepped out of the way as the attacker swung at him. No way was he letting this man get away again.

Graham punched the attacker in the stomach and followed it with a blow to his chest, which took the wind out of his assailant. The man tilted forward as he wheezed in air. Graham grabbed the man's arm and bent it behind his back while at the same time securing his free arm around the man's neck to restrain him.

The man fought to break free, shifting and angling his body. Graham tightened his hold on him. He was exhausted from the pursuit and his earlier injuries, and he wasn't sure how much longer he could keep the man under control. Despite the winter chill, sweat ran down his face.

Graham breathed a sigh of relief when he heard sirens in the distance. The suspect's struggle to break free had grown half-hearted and then stopped altogether.

"It's over," said Graham, and he marched the attacker around the pallets and out toward the street.

Officer Zetler had just emerged from the subdivision. When he saw Graham with the attacker in custody, he stopped to talk on his radio, probably to let the police know where to find them.

Within minutes, a police car showed up. After he'd been read his rights, the attacker was cuffed and taken away. Now they would find out who he was. Maybe knowing his identity would clarify if the two cases were connected and if the cartel was involved.

Graham and the officer walked back toward the hospital. As satisfied as he was with the capture, he wasn't sure if it meant that Marielle and Ian were any safer. If the man was a hired assassin, the forces behind these attacks might just send someone else.

TWELVE

Marielle sat on the floor of the interview room in the police station with Ian. One of the officers had supplied her with a box filled with toys and books meant to help young children feel comfortable before they were questioned.

Ian took a drink from his juice box and leaned against her shoulder as she read a picture book to him.

There was a gentle knock on the slightly ajar door and Graham spoke up. "Can I come in?"

She cleared her throat. "Sure," she responded, feeling a tightening through her torso.

Graham entered holding a small laptop. Once Graham had been released from the hospital, they'd gone to the police station and had agreed upon a plan for questioning Ian in a way that would cause him the least amount of stress. She explained that they needed to set up an environment where Ian felt safe, taking time to play with him and then casually introducing the questions they needed answered.

She hoped it worked. The second Ian showed any sign of distress, she would pull the plug on the interview.

Ian's face brightened when he saw Graham. A light came into Graham's eyes as well. He sat down on the floor beside the boy.

It seemed that Ian trusted both her and Graham now. Rather than have a police officer be a part of the interview, having the two of them work together in a relaxed environment would create the best circumstances for getting answers from Ian. The interview room with only a table and chairs was less than ideal but the snacks, books and toys helped.

"We're almost done with this story," said Marielle. She finished the last couple of pages, locking gazes with Graham when she closed the book. She said a quick, silent prayer.

Please, God, protect this little one's heart and mind.

Graham gave her a slight nod and opened up the laptop. "Ian, can you look at some pictures for me?"

Ian put his juice box down and nodded, gazing up at Graham who was tapping on the keyboard of the laptop.

Marielle leaned closer to Ian. She and Graham had talked through this plan at length. Ian might be able to shed light on the nature of the relationship between his dad and uncle, David and Charlie. More importantly, they needed to find out if the man Graham had taken into custody, who they now knew was named Lee Masters, was the man who had killed Ian's mother.

The first photograph came up on the screen. It was of Charlie Roane.

"Do you know this man?" Graham put his finger on the screen.

Ian nodded.

As planned, Marielle asked the second question. "Was he ever at your house with your mommy and daddy?"

Again, Ian nodded. She wasn't picking up on any distress from the child. Every question had to be phrased for Ian to give a yes or no answer. Though he had uttered that one word over concern for Graham, she couldn't count on him speaking now.

The idea was to tag team easier warm-up questions until they got to the question about the killer's identity.

"Was he nice to you?"

Ian nodded.

"Was he nice to your mom and dad?" Graham's question.

Ian let out a little breath but then nodded. His forehead crinkled. Perhaps he wanted to give a more nuanced answer.

She had to try. "Is there anything else

you want to tell us about this man?"
Maybe he would talk.

Ian wiggled and then drew his knees up
toward his chest before shaking his head.
It wasn't clear from the question what
the nature of the relationship between the
brothers was. Charlie had been to David's
house, so the brothers weren't estranged.

"Did you ever see this man fighting
with or yelling at your mom or dad?"
She was impressed. Graham had come
up with a way to phrase the question so
that Ian might be able to respond.

Ian shook his head.

Progress. It seemed the relationship between the brothers had not been antago-
nistic.

"Good job, Ian." Marielle ruffled his
hair. "You still have some crackers left
in this package. Would you like one?"
She reached for the snack Ian had been
munching on earlier.

They let Ian eat his snack for a few

minutes before they moved onto the next photograph and the harder questions.

"I have another picture I want to show you. Is that okay?" After Ian gave the go-ahead, Graham brought up the picture of the man who had come after them at the camp. It had taken the police only a quick search to find out that Lee Masters was a local who had been arrested for drug use. Lee had returned to the area a few years ago after fifteen years in the army. Police had been unable to get any information out of Lee while he sat in a jail cell, though the drug history suggested a motive for why he might have killed Kristen.

The sight of the photograph of Lee caused Ian to stop chewing his cracker.

"We know this man was not nice to you or me when we were at the camp in the mountains." Marielle wrapped her arm around Ian. "But he's not going to hurt you anymore. The police locked him away because he was bad." Ian's body softened against her.

Graham piped up. "Ian, can you be brave and answer some questions for us about this man?"

Ian glanced at Graham and then nodded before taking another nibble of his snack.

Marielle tried to relax as she prepared to ask the next question. "Do you remember the night a bad thing happened in your house?"

Ian's body tensed but he managed a nod.

Graham pointed at the screen. "Was this man there that night?"

She flinched, concerned that Graham had asked the final question a little too fast.

Ian took the last bite of his cracker. She listened to the sound of his chewing as the seconds ticked by. Graham leaned closer to him as the little boy stuck his fingers in his mouth. Ian stared at the screen for a long moment before shaking his head.

She pointed to the screen. "You're sure this man was not at your house?"

Ian gazed up at Marielle and then nodded.

Graham closed the laptop. "You did good, buddy."

They had their answer. Lee had not killed Ian's mom.

Ian stood up and crawled into Marielle's lap, resting his head against her chest. She rocked back and forth and stroked his hair. "Thank you so much, Ian. I bet you're tired now, huh?"

She offered Graham a faint smile. She was pretty worn out as well. Graham still looked a little pale, probably because his injuries were still hurting him. Most likely the chase after Lee had set him back. Neither of them seemed to want to move.

Ian nodded off in her arms.

"That was helpful, huh?" she whispered.

"Yes, we learned quite a bit. Lee was probably hired by whoever killed Kristen to kidnap Ian and hand him off to Kristen's killer."

She did not want to speculate what would have happened to Ian after that. The implications led to places she didn't want to think about. "So Lee was hired by someone who took a risk in killing Kristen and didn't want to pop up on the radar again. Someone with money and connections, like a cartel member?"

He nodded. "I need solid evidence, but I don't think the timing with what happened with the brothers and Ian's mom is a coincidence."

"A shipment of drugs belonging to the cartel leaves Mexico and disappears. A few days later, the sister-in-law of the driver is killed."

"I think the killer went to the Roanes' house looking for answers about the shipment knowing that David and Charlie were brothers and when he didn't get them, he got angry. The murder was impulsive."

She checked that Ian was completely asleep in her arms. "Kristen died. David feared for his life and went into hiding. We don't know what happened to Charlie."

Graham nodded. "We still have lots of dots to connect. In any case, I think we'll have to work more closely with the local police to try to make the connections we need to make."

"Thank you for helping me do the interview with Ian." She appreciated that Graham wanted to protect Ian as much as she did.

He pressed his shoulder against hers. "We make a good team."

His proximity made her heart flutter. The way he was so good with Ian heightened her attraction to him. What was going to happen next? Would he be leaving her and Ian to pursue the investigation? The notion should have brought her relief but instead sadness washed over her. "If you think someone hired Lee, that means Ian and I are not safe." Her breath hitched when she spoke the words.

Ian snored softly.

"Yes, we'll have to see what the police can set up to ensure your safety." He leaned back against the wall. "I'll help transport the two of you if they come up with a secure location."

"And then what?" It sounded like his intent was to leave them there. "I imagine you're going to tackle this investigation head-on."

He didn't answer right away. "Yes, I guess that's the next step for me." His words came out haltingly as if he were still mulling over what his next move was.

There was a knock on the door. Detective Strickland, the man who was in charge of investigating Kristen's murder, popped his head in. "I've got some things to talk to you two about."

"I need to lay Ian down somewhere first," said Marielle.

The detective opened the door wider. "There's a couch in the break room."

Graham stood up and reached down toward Marielle. "Here, let me take him." She transferred the listless Ian into his arms.

They followed Detective Strickland down a hallway. Marielle watched as Graham gently laid Ian on his side on the couch and then removed his coat to cover the boy, touching his silky blond head lightly.

The picture of Graham gazing down at Ian, how tender he was toward him, pulled on her heartstrings.

They tiptoed out of the room where the detective was waiting. He was a tall man in his forties with a mustache and widow's peak. From the beginning, he'd been supportive of Marielle's need to protect Ian, even if it slowed the investigation.

"Let's talk just outside this room," Marielle whispered. "If he wakes up, I'll be able to hear him. I don't want him to be scared because he's alone."

The detective nodded and fiddled with the folder he was holding before he addressed Marielle. "First, I wanted to let you know that Kristen and David's house is no longer a crime scene. If you wanted to get some more of Ian's things to help him adjust, that would be fine."

"It's clear Lee did not act alone," said Graham. "I don't want either Marielle or Ian out in the open. We think this might connect to a case I'm working that has wider-reaching implications."

"I've been briefed on your case," said Detective Strickland.

"I have to be the one to go to the house," Marielle responded. "I understand what to get from the home to facilitate him talking again and to help him with the transition of being with me."

The detective turned toward Graham. "Maybe you can go with Marielle once we take Ian to the secure location. There will be a female officer there to help with the childcare."

Graham looked at Marielle as if waiting for an answer from her.

"I suppose that would be all right."

Graham turned toward Detective Strickland. "Was there something else? You said it affected the investigation."

"Yes, it's the reason we went ahead with the safe house setup. Lee finally admitted to not acting alone but he won't say who hired him. Honestly, I think he's scared."

She shuddered. Yet another reason to believe they were dealing with big players with lots of power.

The detective held up the folder. "Another piece of the puzzle. We pulled Lee's financials. The guy owns a knife sharpening business, and he's about to be fore-closed on."

Graham nodded. "So he had motive. He needed a big payday."

"Not only that. A day before that storm hit, he deposited five thousand dollars." He handed the folder to Graham. "Everything we know about him so far."

Marielle crossed her arms over her chest, trying not to relive the violence that had happened because of Lee. "He probably thought it would be easy to take out a woman and kidnap a child living alone in the country."

"Well, you proved him wrong." Admiration filled Graham's voice as he reached out to squeeze her arm.

"The five thousand is probably just a portion of his pay," said the detective. "He would have gotten the rest if he'd succeeded. I've got some more work to do. I'll let you both know when we're ready to transport you to the safe house."

"I'll need a vehicle to take Marielle to Ian's house."

"We can arrange that." The detective headed back down the hall and disappeared around a corner.

Graham sat down in a chair in the hallway and opened the folder.

She sat down beside him. "Anything in there that Strickland didn't already tell you?"

Graham scanned the pages as he flipped through them. "Lee has extensive firearms experience and a black belt."

Though he was not a professional hit man, Lee clearly had skills.

She and Ian had come so close to dying at Lee's hands. An outcome that could have been very different if Graham had not been at the camp. Graham returning to the place he felt close to God after Cesar's death had saved her and Ian's life.

Marielle rose and wandered farther down the hall to a window. Outside, the snow twirling down from the nighttime sky created a peaceful scene. The calm she saw outside stood in contrast to the turmoil she was experiencing on the inside.

It appeared that she and Ian were far from safe.

Graham's stomach clenched as he pulled up to the house where Ian had lived with his mom and dad. So far since Lee had been taken into custody, no additional attacks had happened. How long would it take for whoever had hired Lee to line up another assassin?

The place was in need of paint, and car parts and broken toys half covered in snow were scattered through the yard. The house was on the outskirts of town with other older homes on large lots.

"Did his mom and dad own this house?"

"I think it belonged to a relative who let them live there for cheap," said Marielle.

Last night, he and Marielle had gotten Ian settled at the safe house and all of them had gotten a good night's sleep. In the morning in the unmarked police car he'd borrowed, he'd driven Marielle to her place to pick up some clothes and other necessities for her and Ian before coming to Ian's old house.

The more time he spent with Ian, the fonder he grew of him. "What's going to happen with Ian anyway? Are you going to adopt him?"

"Likely not if his father is found. I don't know what David's involvement with the stolen truck is. It takes a lot to sever parental rights. Of course I'm open to adopting him. I'd have the family I always wanted." Her words were tinged with sadness.

"No matter what, I just hope the little guy has a shot at a decent life."

"Me too." Marielle unbuckled her seat belt. "I'll try not to take too long."

"I'm coming with you," he said.

"I should be okay, don't you think?" She glanced nervously toward the house.

He pushed open his door. "Let's not take any chances."

A chill settled over his skin as they made their way through the yard. Marielle used the key the police had given her. Once inside, the scent of ammonia reached him. Crime scene clean-up had done their job. Even though there was no visible sign of what had taken place, stepping into the house gave him an unsettled feeling the way visiting a crime scene always did.

"What are you looking for, anyway? You got the clothes he needs from your place."

She moved through the living room, reaching for a photograph of a woman on a shelf. "Anything that might help unlock Ian's ability to speak. Anything that might comfort him and create a sense of familiarity and safety." She put the photograph in the bag she'd brought with her.

The picture must be of Ian's mother. He stepped toward the shelf, noticing a photo of Ian being held by Kristen, both of them smiling. "Take this one too."

She placed the second photo in her bag. "I'm going to check in Ian's room. Let me know if you find anything that you think might be helpful."

He wandered toward the kitchen where the strong ammonia smell was coming from.

The photos hanging on the living room wall caught his attention. Several of them were of Charlie and David dressed in camo gear and holding bows, their arms wrapped around each other. More evidence that the brothers were close. Still, where an addict was involved, brother could turn against brother.

When he stepped into the kitchen, the floor gleamed in contrast to the dusty, uninhabited feel of the rest of the place. The murder must have happened in this room. He glanced around trying to picture what had happened. Ian could have hidden behind the wall in the living room and then run to hide under the bed where he'd been found.

Cups and bowls still sat in the dishrack, and a loaf of bread and some canned goods had been left on the counter. A sadness washed over him. No one would be returning to straighten up anytime soon. The sight of a child's wooden puzzle on the kitchen table with pieces scattered around it only added to the sense that something had been irrevocably broken.

A muffled banging noise caught his attention. He straightened his spine as his heart beat a little faster. The sound was coming from the backyard. Could be a door caught in the wind.

He went through the kitchen to the back porch. Outside, the doors of a metal shed were open, and someone was throwing items out onto the snow-covered lawn.

His first thought was that an enterprising neighbor had decided to take advantage of the house being abandoned to find things of value.

"Hey, what are you doing?"

The noise stopped. A man stuck his head out.

Graham froze as he looked into the face of Charlie Roane.

"This is my brother's place. I have the right to be here."

"Charlie Roane. I think you better come with me. The police have some questions to ask you." Graham's gun was hidden in a shoulder holster.

The man stepped out of the shed with his hands up. He was a tall, thin man with almond-shaped eyes and stringy brown hair. He was dressed in camouflage gear. "Am I in trouble? I told ya. This is my brother's place. Are you with children's services? Where is Ian at?"

Graham advanced toward Charlie. He pulled his badge and showed it. "We just need to talk to you about your brother." So far, Charlie seemed to want to cooperate. Drawing his weapon might scare Charlie off. No need to say anything about the truck from Mexico. He didn't want to clue the guy in that the police knew what he was guilty of.

"So you're with the police?" Charlie kept his hands up but shuffled his feet, growing more agitated. His gaze bounced all over the place.

"We just have some questions to ask you."

Charlie dropped his hands and took off running. Graham raced after him across a field toward a dirt road.

He ran faster when he saw Charlie approaching a car. Charlie jumped into the vehicle. Graham could hear the engine sputter to life just as he got to the car and reached for the driver's side door handle. It was locked.

The car sped out onto the road.

Graham spun around when he heard another car behind him. Marielle was behind the wheel of the borrowed car. He jumped into the passenger seat.

Even before he had time to close the door, she was rolling forward. He clicked into his seat belt. A bulging bag sat on the console between them.

"I saw from the bedroom window what was going on. I figured he had a car close by and would try to get away."

"Good thinking." He pulled his phone out and dialed the police department to let them know what was going on and maybe get some backup.

"I'll talk to dispatch," said the police officer who answered. "See if we have any officers in the area that could intercept him."

"Might want to send an officer over to the house. The guy was looking for something in the shed in the backyard. I don't think he found it before fleeing."

Graham stared out the windshield where Charlie's car had taken a turn that led into a forested area. He advised the officer of where they were going and disconnected.

Marielle navigated the rutted dirt road with skill. Because of all the curves, the other car was no longer visible. She gripped the wheel and kept a steady speed. They couldn't be far behind.

He wasn't familiar with this area. The sign as they had turned in had said they were on National Forest land and that there was a campground up ahead.

"Where do you suppose he's going?"

She shook her head. "He must have an escape route in mind."

She kept driving. Even when the road straightened out, they saw no sign of the other car. They passed the campground, which was empty.

She slowed down. "I think we lost him. He must've turned off somewhere."

The road appeared to end at the campground.

She turned the car around and headed back down the mountain. Graham scanned both sides of the road looking for any sign of where Charlie might have turned off the road. He saw only forest and rugged hills, no side roads.

Marielle drove even slower. "He couldn't just vanish into thin air."

Graham caught a flash of color in his peripheral vision. "Stop. Back up."

She shifted into Reverse. The car Charlie had been driving was a shade of gray that would blend into the surroundings so it would be hard to spot.

Graham scanned the forest where he thought he'd seen something out of place. Except where the evergreens provided canopy, snow covered much of the ground. "Pull over." He pointed to where he wanted her to park.

She backed up onto the shoulder.

Other than some flattened grass, he didn't see anything that would clearly indicate that Charlie had gone down into this part of the forest.

When she moved to unbuckle her seat

belt, he put a protective hand on her leg. "Stay here."

"Are you sure? If he tries to jump you, it will be two against one if I go."

Maybe she was right. If Charlie had had a gun, he would have used it when he first saw Graham at the house. At least they would not be confronting an armed man. "All right. Let's go."

He pulled his gun from the holster. They exited the car and walked down the hill toward the forest. Just inside the tree line, Graham saw more clearly what had caught his eye. There was a sort of makeshift winter camp, a tent covered by a lean-to made of evergreen branches that not only protected it from the elements but concealed it as well. Only patches of the tent, which was blue, were visible. That must have been what had caught his eye from the road.

A ring of rocks surrounding coals indicated a fire had been built at some point. After signaling for Marielle to step back,

Graham stood off to one side of the tent and pulled back the flap, revealing a sleeping bag on a bed of boughs along with some canned goods and a cooking pot. He straightened and walked around to the back of the camp, peering deeper into the woods. No sign of Charlie or his car. The guy had to have parked somewhere.

A high-speed whizzing sound filled the air and then Marielle screamed.

Fearing the worst, he sprinted around to the front of the tent as his heart pounded in his chest.

THIRTEEN

Marielle barely had time to react to the arrow that had whizzed past her face and embedded in a tree trunk, before a second arrow came at her. Graham pushed her to the ground before the arrow could find its target. She hit the earth hard, landing on her stomach. Pine needles poked at her palms and belly.

He rolled off her and pushed himself up, glancing back and forth. "Stay low. Get to the car." He held his gun in one hand.

She sprinted in the direction of the car, staying in the cover of the forest. Graham was right behind her. Another arrow shot out in front of them. They both zigzagged, stepping behind the thick trunk of an evergreen. She leaned against the tree, trying to catch her breath and slow her raging heart.

Graham angled around the tree, probably trying to locate where the archer was. "I don't see him, but we have to assume he's still stalking us."

Charlie had been dressed in winter camo clothes. It would be easy enough to conceal himself.

The final sprint to the car would be out in the open. As though they were about to plunge into a deep pool, they nodded at each other and burst out into the snow-covered grassy area below the road.

Her feet pounded the earth as she ran. Graham came up beside her, creating a barrier between her and where the archer probably was. When they got to the car, she flung open the passenger side door just as an arrow hit the window and bounced off.

Graham shot his gun in the direction

the arrow had come from before running around to the other side of the car.

Gasping for breath, she crawled in and slammed the door.

He got behind the wheel. Before she even had her seat belt on, he'd pulled the car forward and performed a three-point turn in the small space the shoulder provided so the car faced downhill, the direction they'd come from.

As the tires started rolling, she glanced behind her and then down the hill to the campsite. The archer kept himself well hidden.

"Call the police. They must be on this road, somewhere close by. This whole area needs to be searched. He's hidden his car somewhere."

She pulled out her phone but stopped when she looked through the windshield and saw the police car coming toward him. "Guess you can tell him in person."

Both Graham and the officer rolled down their windows when the two vehicles pulled up side by side. Graham explained the situation.

"We can get forest service involved in the search as well," said the officer before grabbing his radio.

"We need to take him into custody. He's an important player in a case I'm working on," Graham added.

The officer had turned his attention to talking on the radio to get more help.

"I'm not taking any more chances." Graham rolled up his window and edged around the other car on the narrow road. "I'm taking you back to the safe house."

By the time they got down to the main road, her heartbeat had slowed, and she could catch her breath. No matter where she turned, someone wanted her dead. Fear prickled over her skin and she shuddered when she thought about how close the arrow had come to piercing her. "I wonder if Charlie knows that I'm the one taking care of Ian. Why would he want to kill me?"

Graham slowed down on the icy road. "I think he was just trying to protect himself from being taken in by the police. He figured out I was law enforcement. He probably thought you were too."

Graham settled his focus on the road, which was bordered by forest on both sides. The chase had taken them at least five miles outside of town.

A car from a side road pulled in front of them, appearing suddenly from behind some trees. Graham braked and then kept his foot off the gas, going slow until the other vehicle was able to speed up.

As distance grew between the two cars, it took a moment for it to register that she'd seen the car before. "Graham, that car looks like—" Everything had happened so fast when they'd first encountered Charlie. She'd only glimpsed the car he was driving.

Graham had seen the car when he was on foot and for longer. "I think you're right."

The other car disappeared around a curve.

"There must be more than one way off that mountain that leads back to the highway," she said.

Her hand gripped the sides of her seat as the other car came back into view again only much farther ahead of them now. Several cars going in the opposite direction whizzed by them. "We have to go after him." The police were probably still searching the mountain and the camp where Charlie had last been seen.

Graham kept his eyes on the road. "Call the police and let them know where we are."

Graham hung back but kept the other car within view. Charlie's car sped past the exit that would lead back into Clarksville.

She held the phone in her hand. "Where do you suppose he's headed if he's not going back to town?"

"Not sure. He doesn't seem to be aware that he's being followed so far."

She pressed in the number for Detective Strickland and asked him to relay the message to the officer they'd encountered headed up the mountain and let him know what was going on.

The officer called them a few minutes later. "It's going to take me a while to get back down to the main road. I got some forest service people up here helping me search. I'll radio and see if there is anyone closer. Highway patrol might be able to help. You don't know where he's going?"

"No, he passed the exit that would have taken him back into Clarksville."

"Keep us apprised of the situation. Tell Graham not to try to take him in on his own."

When she glanced in his direction, Graham had a laser-like focus on the road and the other car. "Will do." She ended the call.

She had a feeling Graham was not going to wait for backup.

They passed a road sign that listed the next three towns they would encounter. Two of them were less than a thousand people, but the third was Bozeman, which was a city of more than fifty thousand, and fifteen miles away.

"Do you think maybe he's trying to get to the airport in Bozeman?"

Graham flexed his hands on the steering wheel. "Could be. After encountering us, things just got too hot for him and he's looking to escape."

"Funny he didn't leave sooner though. If he was able to sell the drugs, why not get out of town fast?"

"Maybe he wasn't able to sell the drugs." Graham shrugged. "Or something else kept him here."

As the road straightened out, the distance between the two cars shrank.

Marielle tensed. They'd gotten close enough to the other car for her to see that

Charlie was not alone in the car. He had a passenger. Earlier when Graham had been trying to avoid an accident when he'd first pulled out on the road, she'd only been paying attention to the car and hadn't noticed the other person.

Graham slowed down. "I don't want him to figure out he's being tailed."

There were enough other cars headed toward Bozeman so they would not stand out.

Graham slowed so that there was a car between him and the one he was tailing.

The gray car took the exit that would lead to the airport without signaling first, as did the car that was between them, a dark blue SUV. Graham turned as well.

They went through a series of three roundabouts with traffic merging from four different directions.

She scanned the lanes of traffic. "I don't see him anymore."

"He's got to be here somewhere." Once at the airport, Graham found parking close to the departure doors. "If they aren't already inside, they will be shortly. Let's see if we can catch them."

She pushed open her car door. As they walked toward the building, she noticed the dark blue SUV parking. A tall blond man and a shorter bald man got out.

There was something vaguely familiar about the short man.

Graham came up beside her as the doors slid open. "I'll look for Charlie and his passenger. You try and find a security officer."

The departure lines for several of the carriers were quite long. She did not see Charlie anywhere. She hurried across the carpet in search of a security officer. When she glanced over her shoulder, Graham had been eaten up by the crowd.

Again, she spotted the tall blond man and his shorter colleague. The short man made eye contact with her for just a second.

Her heart thumped. Now she knew

where she'd seen him. He was the man from the hospital who had set the trap for Lee to get at her, the man whose arm had been in a sling. Only now, his injury was miraculously healed.

Recognition spread across his face as well. He tugged on the tall blond man's sleeve to get his attention.

Marielle turned to run back to where she'd last seen Graham. When she looked over her shoulder, the short man was running after her.

The number of people in line to talk to agents and check luggage at departures had increased even more. Graham squeezed through clusters of people as he studied the faces of each person he passed. Charlie had been dressed in a camouflage coat with no bright colors on to distinguish him.

Graham continued to search, taking only a few steps at a time. He slowed down even more when a large man bumped his shoulder and then apologized. The collision had caused him to draw his focus away from the lines of people waiting to talk to agents. He turned in a half circle.

A man at a kiosk drew his attention because of his nervous gestures, shifting from foot to foot with his head lowered at an extreme angle as if he was trying to conceal his face. But unless Charlie had changed his clothes, it wasn't him. This man wore jeans, a denim shirt and a gray winter jacket. When Graham noticed that the man didn't appear to have any luggage, he moved in closer.

The man must have sensed someone staring because he looked up suddenly. Graham slipped behind a pillar but not before he saw the man's face. He had only seen photographs of David Roane at his home. He looked a lot like his brother. David must have been the passenger in the car with Charlie. Had they both been hiding out in the woods?

When he stepped out from the cover of the pillar, David was no longer at the kiosk. Graham's adrenaline surged as he glanced around. Where had he gone? It was clear the two men were trying to escape together.

Graham's heart rammed against his rib cage. He couldn't let them get on a flight. He scanned the entire area, face after face, but didn't see them. Then his gaze caught on two men waiting by the elevator. From the back, one looked like Charlie. He pushed through the crowd as the doors opened and the men stepped in. He arrived at the elevator just as the doors closed. The airport only had two floors, so he dashed to the nearby escalator, taking the steps two at a time to reach the concourse.

The second floor consisted of seating areas and offices on one side. The TSA line took up most of the floor. Restaurants, shops and gates were on the other side of the TSA line but visible through windows.

He searched the crowd waiting in line. His targets would have to be toward the end of the line. Though he could not see every person clearly, none of them looked like David or Charlie. He wandered away, still scanning for the two men. Through the windows, he could see people who had cleared TSA and were headed toward gates. No way could they have already gotten through that line.

When he moved to go back to the TSA line, he noticed a tall blond man. Something stood out about him, the way he was swiveling his head around slowly. He also seemed to be searching for someone.

Adrenaline pumped through his body as he walked briskly, surveying the open office doors and the sitting areas. When he moved past the huge open stairway that led back down to the first floor, he caught sight of Charlie just as the man reached the bottom and turned left.

Graham bolted down the stairs. He arrived at the bottom in time to see Charlie and David across the airport. They opened a door and an alarm split the air. They slipped through it as Graham raced past baggage claim, slowed down by a throng of people who had just disembarked and were milling by the carousels. The alarm intensified as he got closer, and he saw they'd made use of an emergency exit.

He glanced around. He had not seen or heard from Marielle for at least ten minutes. There was no time to try to contact her by phone.

He pushed open the door. The cold wind hit him as he stared out at the tarmac filled with planes and personnel loading, unloading and hauling luggage, along with men and women in reflective clothing directing airplane traffic. The intense rumble of a plane about to take off filled the air. There was a barrier that the two men would have had to jump in order to get out on the tarmac. They must have gone in some other direction.

On his other side looked to be a number of smaller, private planes, and he saw two men disappearing around a private hangar. Graham took off running, following the route around the hangar the men had gone. He ran past a second building that butted up against a scraggly field of low shrubs.

He glanced around. Several men were standing outside an open hangar working on a small plane. Tools were scattered across the concrete. He looked in the other direction. A group of maybe ten people stood beside a small plane while they loaded their own luggage. No sign of David or Charlie anywhere, though there were a couple of places they could've hidden.

The wind and the noise of an airplane lifting into the sky just fifty feet above him drowned out all other noise.

His attention was drawn back to the

field. He saw a makeshift path where enough people had trod to create a way through the shrubs. All the same, the field looked like a tangled maze of plant life.

The control tower for the private planes would provide him with a view of most of this area. He ran toward it, finding the door marked *Authorized Personnel Only* unlocked, and he rushed up the stairs where a man and woman sat in front of monitors.

The man whirled his chair around. "Hey, you're not supposed to be up here."

Graham pulled his badge. "DEA. I need to have a look at this area through your windows."

The man nodded. "We've got twenty minutes before another plane takes off. Go ahead."

The windows of the tower provided him with a 360-degree view of the area. He was able to see most of the possible hiding places. No sign of David or Charlie anywhere, but by the edge of the field, he spotted that same tall blond man he'd seen before. The man looked like he was headed back toward the commercial airport. His breath caught. What was going on with that guy?

His eyes came to rest on an open area in the field. He leaned closer to the window, trying to see better. "Do you have binoculars?"

The woman opened a drawer and handed a pair to him. Graham peered through the lenses that magnified what he was seeing. There on the ground in the field lay Charlie and David. Charlie was motionless and prone, a crimson stain evident on his back. Partially sitting up, David clutched his stomach and then collapsed.

Graham's chest squeezed tight. "Call 911. I think we have a possible homicide and attempted murder over in that field." And the tall blond man was the number one suspect. Fear gripped his heart as he realized the blond man was headed back to the commercial part of the airport— and Marielle.

FOURTEEN

"I have a gun. I think you better come with me."

Marielle's heart pounded as the short bald man gripped her arm and pressed something against her back.

The short man spoke his threatening words with his mouth close to her ear. Minutes before, while she'd searched for Graham, she'd managed to initially elude the man, but he'd caught her by surprise by flanking around a crowd. Thinking she was getting away, she'd almost run into him, and he'd grabbed her.

Squeezing even tighter, he yanked on her arm. "Come on."

Her breath came out in shallow gasps as her gaze darted everywhere and she tried to come up with a plan of escape. People milled around her—some waited at baggage claim while others went into shops or stood in line to talk to airline agents.

Marielle didn't think he would shoot her in front of witnesses. She needed to stay where there were people. Once the short man led her to someplace secluded, he probably intended to kill her.

She was sure the pair of men had been tailing Charlie, just like she and Graham had. She also knew the short man was the same person who'd set her up so Lee could get at Ian at the hospital. Did these two men work for the cartel?

Still trying to come up with a plan, she spoke softly to him. "Did Charlie Roane betray you and take drugs that belonged to you?"

"Look, lady, I just follow orders." He yanked her arm, leading her toward an exit.

She planted her feet. Going outside would make her more vulnerable. "Is the tall blond guy your partner or your boss?"

"My boss. You ask too many questions. Let's go." He pushed the gun into her spine, though she barely felt it through the thickness of her winter coat. His chest pressed close to her back to conceal the gun from other people. "Where's the kid at anyway?" His grip on her arm tightened. He shoved her toward the door that led outside.

They were still trying to get to Ian. "He's safe."

Marielle knew she had to get away and fast. Pulling herself free of his grip, she whirled around. While he fumbled to conceal the gun, she pushed him and shouted, "I told you to stay away from me. After all you put me through, I don't love you anymore. I'm going to Vegas with Phil."

The groups of people close to them all looked in her direction. The short man had managed to stuff the gun in a pocket before anyone saw it. His face was flushed with rage, or was it embarrassment? She couldn't tell.

The short man reached to grab her coat sleeve.

Another man stepped between them. "Hey, man, leave the lady alone. She made it clear she doesn't want to be with you."

"Yeah, listen to him," said a woman.

She took a step back.

While everyone was still watching their interaction and the short man was prevented from getting at her, she thanked the man who had intervened and stalked away. She still did not know what had happened to Graham, or to Charlie and his passenger.

Pushing down the rising sense of panic, she scanned the area, hoping to see a security guard or Graham. When she saw neither, she pulled out her phone to call Graham. She was about to slip into the safety of a crowded gift shop when the tall blond man, the one who was apparently the boss, entered the airport from outside.

He spotted her right away.

As if a weight was placed on her chest, fear made it hard to breathe. She darted into the gift shop and worked her way toward the back of the store. When she lifted her head, she had a partial view of the blond man standing at the threshold of the store searching for her. He towered above the other people. Her heart pounded as she slipped behind a display of paperback books.

Her phone vibrated in her pocket. Graham.

"Hello." She spoke in a low voice.

The blond man had entered the store.

"Where are you?" Graham sounded out of breath.

She moved away from the paperback display toward a group of people reading greeting cards. The blond man was tracking her with his gaze edging in her direction. She hurried to get away from him.

"I just stepped out of the first floor gift shop." She kept walking, knowing that the blond man would be behind her. "A tall blond man is after me."

"I'm familiar with him. I'm coming toward you as fast as I can," said Graham.

Her head was down as she talked on the phone. She bumped a man's shoulder. "Oh, sorry."

"I bet you are," came a voice filled with intense sarcasm.

When she looked up, it was the short man. Her breath caught and she tensed up. She turned in the opposite direction. The blond man was closing in on her. Her heart skipped into overdrive.

Outside there was a cacophony of noise as several police cars with sirens blaring whizzed past. Had Graham called the police? Why? The blond man fixated on the police cars outside, shaking his head. He backed away, disappearing into the crowd. When she looked around, she did not see the short man either.

Graham's voice came across the line. "I see you."

She looked up. A cluster of people cleared a path. Graham was standing not more than twenty feet from her. She rushed over to him, and he gathered her into his arms.

"I'm so glad to see you." Her hand brushed over his flannel shirt. "Two men were after me."

"I know." He took her hand. "Did you see where they went?"

"They disappeared when the police cars went by."

"The sirens must have scared them away. We need to go talk to the police. Maybe they can be caught before they leave the airport." He took her hand and directed her toward the exit.

"I don't understand. What's going on?"

The sliding doors opened, and they stepped outside. "I have some bad news."

Flashing lights drew her attention to the private airport, where two ambulances and a fire truck had joined the two police cars.

"David was the passenger with Charlie. They both have been shot. We better hurry. Last I saw, David was still alive."

The shock of the news made her light-headed as a numbness set in. The questions reeling through her mind were interrupted when Graham tugged on her sleeve, and they took off running toward the flashing lights. She wondered if the blond man or the short man had had anything to do with Charlie and David being shot. If David died, what would happen to Ian?

She sprinted alongside Graham who directed her around several hangars to a field.

A small crowd had gathered just outside where the police tape had been strung.

Graham showed his badge to the police officer who was making sure the crowd did not encroach on the crime scene. "I'm the guy who called this in. It may connect with a case I'm working."

The officer nodded, and he stepped under the tape. Graham walked over to one of the other officers who was standing at the edge of the field. She couldn't hear what he was saying, but he pointed toward the commercial airport. The officer spoke into the radio on his shoulder, and a second later, two of the officers on the periphery of the crime scene jumped into one of the police cars and drove toward the larger airport.

The EMTs brought a stretcher out of the shrubbery, carrying a body entirely covered in a sheet. Charlie. Her heart sank. The loss of life was always a tragedy, especially when it wasn't clear if the dead man had been able to repent of his choices. She said a prayer for Charlie's soul.

She watched the EMTs load the body into an ambulance. A moment later, a second stretcher carrying David appeared out of the tangle of shrubbery. He was still alive.

She ran toward the stretcher. "David, I'm the woman taking care of Ian."

David's skin looked translucent. Though his eyes were open, he stared at the sky in a listless, unfocused way. "My boy." A brief smile lit up his face.

She grabbed his hand. "He's all right. He's safe."

"Didn't want to leave town without him. Had to hide, stayed…camped near home…"

Graham had come up behind her. "David, was Charlie working for the cartel?"

"No." David gave a tiny shake of his head. "It was supposed to be his big payday. I got a cut for hiding it." He wheezed in a labored breath of air. "Big mistake, cost me everything."

"Did you see the man who killed Kristen?"

David's head jerked as he drew his eyes into a squint that communicated his pain.

The EMT at the head of the stretcher put his hand on Graham's arm. "Agent Flynn, we need to get his man to the hospital."

David closed his eyes. Marielle squeezed his hand before letting go. They got moving, and Graham followed, walking alongside the stretcher. "I have permission to question him."

"I'm sorry. He's critical. We need to go." The EMT looked over his shoulder as they moved past Graham and Marielle. "You can talk to him when he recovers."

"The second he's able to talk, I need to know," said Graham.

Marielle slipped her hand into his. "We need to pray for him."

Graham nodded. "Yes. I want answers about this case, but even more for Ian's sake, I want David to make it."

They stood for a long moment holding hands while they each prayed silently. Both ambulances drove away.

Graham squeezed her hand. "Give me a second to talk to the officer, and then I'll take you back to the safe house."

A cold wind ruffled her hair while she waited. She could see the ambulances in the distance as they wove through the airport toward the exit.

Graham returned after a few minutes. "The police didn't apprehend either of those two men yet."

The news caused her to tense up as she fought to keep the rising fear at bay. "That means they could still come after us."

Marielle's statement had a chilling effect on Graham. "Maybe, but the police think they may have left the airport. They couldn't locate the car I described."

"The parking lot is full, and it's a generic-looking car. They might still be here hiding somewhere."

He'd do anything to ease the concern on her face, the tight jaw and the creased forehead. He pressed his hand against her cheek. "The police will do as much as they can to take those guys in." He wrapped his arm through hers. "Let's get you back to that safe house."

She pressed closer to him as they walked. Snow swirled out of the sky in soft lazy patterns. "Do you suppose those men killed Kristen, or were sent by whoever did?"

"Don't know exactly what their role was."

"The tall blond one seemed to be the one giving orders."

He let out a breath, recalling what he'd seen earlier. "I think the blond guy probably shot David and Charlie. It's clear now from what David said that Charlie stole from the cartel, so it was probably a revenge killing. Maybe they gave up the location of the drugs or the money from the drugs before they were shot."

"Those men came after me too. They know about my connection to Ian," she said. "The short man is the one who tried to trick me at the hospital, and he wanted to know where he was."

"It's Ian they want," said Graham. "They probably know I'm investigating the case and would want me out of the way."

"For sure, the cases are connected now," she said.

"Yes, David implied as much," he said. "My evidence against the blond man is circumstantial. I saw him close to where David and Charlie were gunned down. It's a good enough reason for the police to want to take him in for questioning."

They came to the edge of the larger airport building, moved up the sidewalk and then veered into the parking lot. Graham found himself in a state of hyperawareness as he watched the people around him and the cars pulling out. Those two men were still at large.

She pulled free of his grasp as they

drew nearer to their car. "I hope David makes it." She stopped by the front bumper. "He delayed leaving town because he wanted to take his son with him." Her voice grew soft as she shook her head. "The whole thing is so sad. Regardless of what David has done in his life, he loves his son."

"We don't know David's level of involvement with all of this. What he said to me implied that he was aware of what Charlie had planned and that he stood to benefit by *hiding it*. That could mean the drugs or the money gotten from the drugs."

She nodded. "He might end up going to prison if he does survive the shooting."

"A lot of unknowns right now," he said.

Assuming that the Roane brothers had already sold the drugs, they now knew why they had not gotten out of town right away. The decision had cost Charlie his life.

Marielle and Graham climbed into the borrowed car.

Graham pulled out of the parking space and drove toward the airport exit. Fully aware that they might be followed, he kept his eye on the traffic behind them taking the road that led back out to the highway.

His phone rang. He lifted it from his pocket and glanced at it. One of the police officers he'd been in contact with. He needed to focus on driving, so he handed the phone to Marielle. "Put it on speaker."

She took the phone and pushed the connect button. "This is Marielle. Graham is with me in the car. We have you on speaker."

"Great, just wanted to let you know that we figured out what Charlie was looking for in that shed. It seems he had stashed some money and gold jewelry back there."

"Probably what he made from the sale

of the drugs," said Graham. And he was probably coming to get it so he could get out of town. After Graham had found his camp, Charlie must have convinced David that things were too hot to stay in Clarksville anymore. They needed to leave without Ian.

"One other thing," said the officer. "It looks like there was another camp not too far from the one you and Marielle came upon."

Graham hit his turn signal as he came up to the exit that would lead back to the safe house in Clarksville. "Probably where David was hiding out." Separate camps meant that if one of them got caught or killed, the other might still be able to take the money and escape. "Thanks for the info. Keep me in the loop."

Marielle pressed a button on the phone and handed it back to Graham. He was on one of the main thoroughfares of the city, two lanes of traffic in each direction.

Though he'd never gotten a close look at it, a dark-colored SUV behind him held his attention for some time. He hit his blinker and turned into a gas station.

"Why are we stopping?"

"Need gas."

She leaned to peer at the dashboard. "You have a quarter tank. That's enough to get back to the safe house." She straightened her back, still watching him. Her eyes held a question, waiting for an explanation.

When he looked around the gas station, he didn't see the suspicious car anywhere. He put his hand on hers. "I just don't want to take any chances that we might lead those men to Ian."

She reached up to brush her fingers over his face. "Thank you for caring as much about him as I do."

He smiled. "The kid grows on ya."

"Indeed, he does." She laughed and leaned toward him even more so that their foreheads were almost touching.

Their eyes met as a charge of electricity zinged through him. He wanted to kiss her.

She pulled her hand away from his face and sat up but not before he caught that same warmth in her expression that he'd experienced.

Perhaps it was best that she'd ended the moment. What sort of mixed message would that give her anyway? Once this investigation was over, his job would take him to some other part of the world. From the beginning, his stay in Montana was meant to be temporary.

He shifted into Drive, feeling the flush on his face from the moment of connection between them. "We should get going, huh?"

"Yes, for sure." Her voice was flat, as if she was trying to purge it of any intense emotion.

He waited a few minutes at the gas station before pulling back out on the road. As a precaution, he took a circuitous route to the safe house once he got to Clarksville. Ian was the ultimate target in this dangerous situation, and they had to do everything to protect him.

FIFTEEN

As Graham drove through the subdivision where the safe house was located, Marielle lifted the bag of things she'd gotten from Ian's house and put it on her lap. It felt like a lifetime ago that she'd gathered the items from Ian's house. She hoped something she'd collected would aid in ending Ian's muteness, and she was glad she'd had the presence of mind to hold on to the bag when she'd run out to the car so she and Graham could pursue Charlie.

Graham parked in the car on the driveway by the garage, pulled his phone out and called to let the officers inside know that they were back. A second later, the garage door on the double garage opened up, and he parked the car beside a patrol vehicle.

From the back seat where it'd been tossed, Marielle retrieved the bag of clothes for her and Ian that she'd gotten from her own home.

"It feels like we collected these things a very long time ago," he said, echoing her own earlier thoughts.

"Yes, it does." So much had changed since then. Charlie was dead and David was in critical condition.

Graham cupped his hand on her shoulder.

His touch brought back the memory of the moment of connection they'd shared in the car earlier. She turned to face him. He reached out toward her, indicating he could carry one of the bags. She handed him the bigger, heavier bag of clothes.

When they headed toward the door that connected to the house, he placed his hand on the middle of her back. The gesture may have risen from his instinct to protect her, but still it seemed as though something had shifted between them. He'd almost kissed her in the car earlier.

When Graham opened the door, a police officer, an older man with gray sideburns, was standing several feet from the window that looked out on the street. The gun belt he wore was a reminder of the danger they faced.

Graham stepped aside so Marielle could go in first. She wondered how long it would be before Graham chose to leave her and Ian to become an active part of the investigation. The truth was that she felt safest when she was with him.

She glanced around the room before addressing the older man. "Officer Phelps, where's Ian?"

"He's in the downstairs bedroom with Officer O'Brian." The older man studied Graham for a moment. "Heard you two had a bit of an encounter. Sorry to hear about the shooting. You look like you could use a cup of coffee."

"You go on ahead," Graham told her.

Before stepping into the hallway, she looked over her shoulder at Graham. He was probably anxious to get back out and help with the investigation. She had the protection of two police officers now.

As she stepped toward the bedroom, she heard him say, "I could use a cup, thanks."

She took in a breath that eased the tension in her muscles. He'd be staying for a while anyway.

She entered the downstairs bedroom where Officer O'Brian sat on the floor with Ian while they stacked building blocks. She was a young woman, probably in her early twenties. Her blond hair was pulled up into a tight bun.

Ian gazed up at Marielle and then lifted his hands toward her. She put the bag on the floor and reached for him. "I missed you, little man."

"I'm glad you're back." Officer O'Brian pushed herself to her feet. "I'm going to get a nap upstairs. Officer Phelps and I will be switching off on guard duty, and it would be good if I were rested."

Marielle held Ian and swayed while Ian played with her hair. "That sounds good."

Officer O'Brian left the room.

Marielle put Ian on the bed and reached for the bag of items she'd brought from his home. "Ian, I got you some things you might like. Maybe you can tell me about them."

She drew out the photographs first and pointed at the picture of Kristen. "Who is that? Can you tell me?"

Ian's fingers touched Kristen's smiling face. His lips pressed together as if he was trying to make the "m" sound.

She squeezed his shoulder and patted his back. "Take your time."

He emitted a small abrupt noise then shook his head and flopped down on the bed.

She rubbed his back. "It's all right, Ian.

I know this is hard." She touched the picture again. "It that your mama?"

Ian blinked and then reached out to touch the photograph too before nodding. She couldn't begin to fathom what was going on behind those eyes. His reaction had been calm enough that she guessed he wasn't remembering the violence connected to his mother. Maybe the love and safety he'd known with her was foremost in his developing brain.

Developmentally at his age, he would not necessarily understand that his mom was not coming back.

She pulled out a blanket she'd found in his room. The homemade quilt with squares that featured farm animals looked well loved, with thinning fabric and worn edges. Ian grabbed it and drew it to his chest, resting one cheek against the bed.

"Is that your special blankie?"

He nodded and rubbed a corner of it. She pointed to one of the quilt squares that showed a chicken. Maybe she could get him to talk about something that was less emotionally charged. "Can you tell me what that is?"

He looked at her but did not speak.

"Is it a chicken? What kind of noise does a chicken make?" She had to keep trying to get him to talk.

Ian pressed his lips together as if to make a chicken noise, but no sound came out of his mouth. She tried several other animals on the quilt with the same result, praising him each time he was able to at least mime the noise.

Next she pulled out a stuffed lion and put it behind her back, thinking she would play a game that might help him talk. It too had looked to be in the much-loved and handled category. She'd found it on Ian's bed with the quilt.

"Can you guess who's behind my back? I think he's a friend of yours." She brought the lion out, shook it and made a soft roaring sound.

Ian's countenance changed from relaxed to terrified. He sat bolt upright as his eyes grew round. He shook his head, making a frantic and frightened noise. She dropped the lion and reached for him.

"Ian, it's all right."

He rolled away, crawled to the end of the bed and jumped off. He pulled on his hair.

She got up too, but when she advanced toward him, he made a sound that indicated distress.

Marielle clutched her roiling stomach. Seeing Ian so upset was hard to deal with. This was so unexpected and didn't make any sense.

Graham stood in the doorway holding a coffee cup. "I heard a cry. Everything all right in here?"

"I'm not sure." She slipped the lion back in the bag. "I showed him a toy, a stuffed lion, that I thought would bring him comfort and maybe get him talking. It had the opposite effect."

Graham put his coffee cup on the dresser by the door and rushed over to where Ian crouched in a corner. He dropped down on his knees to be close to the boy but did not reach out toward him. "Hey, buddy, how's it going?" Instead, he waited until Ian moved toward him. After a moment's hesitation, the boy fell into his arms.

Marielle watched as Graham spoke soothing words to him. After a few minutes, Graham rose to his feet and placed a half-asleep Ian on the bed. He sat on the bed and rubbed Ian's back until he fell entirely asleep.

Still shaken by Ian's reaction to the lion, Marielle reached for the quilt and covered Ian with it. She tiptoed toward the door.

After he grabbed his coffee from the dresser, Graham delicately closed the door.

Graham leaned toward her. "How are you doing?" His features filled with concern.

She rubbed her arms, wishing her heart

wasn't still beating so fast. "That was pretty upsetting. I never meant to cause him more pain."

"Why don't you come to the kitchen and we can talk?" He patted her shoulder. "My coffee is cold anyway. I gotta get a fresh cup."

As they walked through the living room, she caught sight of Officer Phelps sitting in an overstuffed chair watching the activity on the street outside.

Graham poured out his now cold coffee into the sink and got a fresh cup from the coffeepot. "You want some?"

"I'm fine. I'll probably catch a nap in a little while." She took a seat at the table, still trying to sort through what had happened. "That is the most agitated I've ever seen Ian. It just doesn't make any sense. That toy was as worn out as the stuffed giraffe he treasures. I found it on his bed along with that quilt I covered him with. He had a positive response to that."

Graham sat down beside her. "He sounded afraid when I heard him cry out from the living room."

"The word I would use to describe his reaction is *terrified*," she said. "Thanks for your help getting him calmed down."

"No problem." He stirred two teaspoons of sugar into his coffee.

"No really, I mean it." She rested her hands on the table and twisted them together. "When I reached out to him, he didn't want me to hold him because he associated me with causing fear. I'm going to have to rebuild trust with him."

"He'll come back around. I'm sure he sees you as a safe person." He placed his hand on hers. "Why do you think that toy scared him?"

The warmth of his touch calmed her. "I'm not sure what's going on. Maybe it's the toy. He associates it with something bad. Maybe it's lions in general. Until he can tell us, we won't know for sure. Showing him a picture of a lion might upset him, and I don't want to put him through that again."

Graham took a sip of his coffee.

"You did so good with him, Graham. You would've been a great dad. You still could be." In the ten years they'd been apart, it seemed that neither of them had moved on into a new relationship and marriage. She wanted him to find a measure of happiness and wondered why he was just as stuck as she was. He was the one who hurt her after all.

His face grew grim as the mood in the room shifted. "I don't know about that." He pushed his chair back and rose to his feet. "I hardly had a good role model for a father."

His words held an intensity she had not heard before. She'd hit a nerve without intending to. "Just because your dad walked out on you and your mom doesn't mean you'd do the same thing."

"He did way worse than that before he left." He turned away from her and gripped the counter. "I just couldn't take a chance having kids. The acorn doesn't fall far from the tree and all that."

When they'd been engaged, they'd talked about having a family. Though Graham had agreed with her about wanting to have children, she remembered that he would often seem sullen and distant after their conversations. Maybe he'd just been agreeable about plans to have a family to make her happy. "Just because your dad wasn't a good father doesn't mean you wouldn't be."

She stared at his back, waiting for him to respond. Tension had descended in the space between them.

"It's not a risk I would want to take with kids of my own. End up ruining their life." He sat his coffee cup on the counter and stared out the window.

"Birth is not destiny, Graham. You could make different choices." This was the first time Graham had ever brought up his fear about repeating the patterns of his father.

"You don't get it, Marielle. You come from a family that has generations of stable parents with a strong faith. I come from the exact opposite."

He stomped out of the room.

Marielle sat at the table in a state of shock.

Graham hurried through the living room toward the front door.

Officer Phelps rose to his feet. "Where are you going?"

"I just need to get some fresh air." The conversation with Marielle had left him feeling shredded. He wanted to be alone.

"I don't think it's a good idea for you to be outside," said the police officer. "If you need some space, there's an office upstairs. Second door on the right."

Graham nodded and rushed up the stairs. The office was sparsely furnished with a desk, rolling chair and mostly empty bookshelf, staged just enough to make it look not like a safe house. He closed the door and plunked down into the chair, swinging it around so he could stare out the window.

Why had Marielle brought up the issue of children and fatherhood? She really didn't get it. She never had. Her mom and dad were great parents.

Years ago, when they'd talked about having a family, he'd had deep insecurities. He'd tried to convince himself that everything would be okay once they were married and a child was born, but the fear would not go away. He just didn't think he was up to the responsibility of fatherhood. He now realized that on an unconscious level, when the recruiter had dangled the offer of an exciting undercover career in front of him, it had allowed him not to have to face his fears.

He rose from the chair to look out the window to the street below. His hand formed a fist, and he pounded it on the windowsill as his jaw grew tight. The truth was he felt a growing connection to Ian that made him afraid on so many levels. He didn't know he could care about a kid that much. The feelings surprised him. But caring didn't mean he had the capacity to parent. The whole thing scared him more than being in a firefight.

If the boy's father recovered and the charges against him were minor, the child would most likely be returned to David. Forming an attachment was not a good idea. Ian's life was in danger. He could lose the little boy just like he'd lost Cesar.

He shook his head.

Everything was so fragile and uncertain.

The conversation with Marielle had been like a collision with his past choices. He'd always thought that a man like him could best serve God by remaining single and focusing on his job. But now, because of his feelings for Marielle and Ian and his disillusionment about his job since Cesar's death, he was beginning to wonder.

He stopped beating his fist on the windowsill and placed his palm on the pane. The bottom line was that no matter what he felt for a child, it didn't mean he'd be a good father. The realization created a chasm inside him.

His job had been so fulfilling for so many years, but now he felt hollow. Maybe if he could focus his energy on closing this investigation, he could get back the solid feeling he got from doing his job as an undercover agent. Time to get some work done.

He made a quick call to Detective Strickland. Police had not been able to locate the two men from the airport. "Look, Marielle and I got a look at both guys. If we can get access to the database of known cartel associates, we might be able to identify them. I can get my boss to help me with that."

"The police officers watching you should have a laptop. It wouldn't hurt to also go through local criminals as well, since that's where Lee Masters was re-cruited from," said Detective Strickland.

"Agreed." Graham held the phone tighter. "Any news on David Roane?"

"No update there. The last I heard was that doctors rushed him into surgery to remove the bullet."

"Interviewing him could give me a lot of answers," said Graham.

"I'll let you know as soon as I hear any-thing."

Graham said goodbye and rushed down-stairs.

If he couldn't interview David, maybe he could figure out who the two men from the airport were.

It took only a few minutes to set up the laptop and get authorization to access the federal database. He invited Marielle to sit beside him while they shuffled through the photographs.

Marielle sat close enough to see the screen they shared. Her shoulder brushed against his when she leaned forward. Her proximity still made his heart beat faster. He narrowed the parameters of the search to blond men over six feet tall.

They combed through dozens of photographs. Each time they shook their heads. After nearly an hour of looking at photographs, his eyes were blurry. He rose to his feet and stretched his arms behind his neck.

Marielle stared at the screen where the last man they'd dismissed was still visible. There were photos of the man's face from the front and the side along with a separate photo showing the distinct tattoo of a dragon on his chest. "Why do they show these pictures of the tattoos?"

"Tattoos and scars are another way to identify a person because they're unique. Tattoos can give a history, as well, if a man has been in prison or part of a gang."

"So the smart thing to do if you were a criminal would be not to get a tattoo," she said.

He laughed and sat back down. "Never thought of it that way, but I suppose you're right. It's part of the criminal culture to put your history and identity on your skin."

Marielle continued to stare at the screen.

His voice filled with concern. "Are you tired? Do you want to take a break?"

She shook her head. "I was just thinking about something. Can you do a keyword search for *lion tattoo*?"

He scooted his chair forward as he processed what she was indicating. "Do you think the man who killed Ian's mom had a lion tattoo and that's why he had such a strong reaction to the toy?"

"It's just a theory."

He pressed the enter button. "Looks

like we have twenty-five matches for men and women with lion tattoos."

He filed through the photographs. At the tenth photo in, she stopped him. "There."

The man they were looking at was not blond and his hair was short. But his facial features resembled that of the tall blond man from the airport and he had a lion tattoo on his arm that would have been covered by his winter coat when they saw him.

He studied the photograph for a long moment. "It could be the same guy. He's just changed his hair color and let it grow out."

Her words held an icy chill. "This might be the man who killed Kristen."

A moan behind him caused him to turn in his seat. Ian had awakened and was holding his blanket.

Marielle shut the laptop and rushed toward Ian to scoop him up. "Hey." She brushed her hand over his hair. "Did you have a good nap?"

Ian nodded.

"Bet you're hungry. Why don't we get you something to eat?"

Graham waited until Marielle disappeared into the kitchen before opening the laptop back up. The man he was looking at had several known aliases, most that were a variation on Georgio Franks. By cross-referencing known associates, he also found a photo of the short bald man who went by the name Eric Smith.

Georgio had lived in different locations throughout the western US. He had some minor drug distribution convictions from years ago. The DEA had connected him to several known cartel members in Mexico. Such a profile suggested he was likely one of the distributors for drugs in the northwest.

He wrote down both names with a brief description by each.

His heartbeat thrummed in his ears as he stared at the photograph. Arched eyebrows and narrowed eyes looked back at him.

Was he looking at Kristen's killer?

SIXTEEN

After seating Ian at the table, Marielle found some wheat crackers in a cupboard. She searched the refrigerator for some more snack possibilities. Grapes caught her eye. She prepared a plate for Ian and placed it on the table in front of him.

After she poured him a cup of milk, she sat down beside him.

He offered her a cracker.

She took it and nibbled. "Thanks, kiddo."

Graham came and stood on the threshold leading into the kitchen. He handed her a piece of paper.

Georgio Franks—tall, blond. Kristen's killer?

Eric Smith—short, bald.

Words did not need to pass between

them. He was probably thinking the same thing as she was. Could they get confirmation from Ian that a man with a lion tattoo had killed his mother?

Ian lifted a grape toward Graham.

Graham sat down in the chair on the other side of the boy and took the grape. "Hey, that looks pretty good." He popped the grape in his mouth and chewed in an exaggerated way, making loud noises.

Ian laughed.

"Are you filling your belly up?" He poked the boy's stomach which made him laugh even louder.

She leaned toward Ian. "We should maybe just make our own snack plate and quit stealing your food."

Ian picked up another cracker and set it in front of her on the table. His sweet nature never ceased to amaze her.

She locked gazes with Graham, lifting her chin slightly to signal that he could ask the questions that needed to be asked. He had a special bond with Ian that might facilitate the boy staying calm when talking about what he'd witnessed. She was still concerned that he might associate her with the lion that had frightened him so much.

Ian placed a cracker and a small bunch of grapes in front of Graham.

"Can I ask you something, buddy?"

Ian nodded and took a bite of his cracker.

"Do you remember the...stuffed animal Marielle showed you?"

Ian stopped chewing for a second. He looked at Marielle, wide brown eyes searching her face.

She put her hand on his back and leaned close to his face. "I didn't mean to make you afraid." Tears rimmed her eyes. "I didn't know it would upset you."

Ian reached up and put his finger close to her eye.

"It's okay." She touched his cheek. "I just don't want you to be afraid. That makes me sad."

He turned his attention back to eating. She listened to the crunching sound of crackers being chewed.

Graham cleared his throat and scooted his chair closer to Ian's. "Would it be okay if we talked about the lion?"

Ian stopped eating, holding his cracker in midair. It took a long moment before he nodded.

"Did the man who hurt your mom have a lion on his skin?"

Ian nodded as he pressed his quivering lips together. Marielle's throat went tight. "It's okay. Graham and I are both here with you. No one is going to hurt you or scare you."

Please, Lord, protect this child's heart and mind.

Graham's words were soft, almost a whisper. "Can you show me where the lion was on the man?"

Ian studied Graham's face for a long moment.

Graham nodded and rested a hand on

Ian's shoulder. "It's okay, little buddy. You can tell me."

Ian touched his upper arm.

The tension eased from her body, and she took in a breath. That confirmed her theory. They most likely knew now who Kristen's killer was, the tall blond man named Georgio.

Ian wiggled in his seat and said, "He was a bad man." He picked up a cracker and took a bite.

Graham looked over Ian's head at Marielle as his mouth dropped open.

Joy burst through her as she drew Ian into a sideways hug. "Indeed." Ian was talking again, and they had a name and face to connect to his mother's killer.

"Come on, how about I read you a story?" said Graham.

Marielle scooted back her chair and rose to her feet. "I'll go get one from the bedroom." She went down the hall and grabbed two books from the top of the stack.

When she came back into the living room, Graham and Ian were sitting on the couch. Officer Phelps had moved to a chair closer to the door. She handed Graham one of the books and then sat on the other side of Ian.

Graham showed Ian the book. "You like this one?"

Ian nodded.

Graham read several pages of the book and then his phone rang. He looked at his phone, his expression growing serious. "I have to take this."

Marielle lifted the book from his hands. "I'll take over."

Graham went into the kitchen to take the call while she read several pages to Ian. He leaned his head against her shoulder.

Graham stepped back into the living room and ushered her over. She got up and walked over to him. After glancing in Ian's direction, he whispered, "David

Roane is out of surgery. I have to go see if I can interview him."

She nodded. "I hope it goes well."

She returned to sit with Ian picking up the book.

Her throat grew tight. It was inevitable that he would have to leave to do his job. They'd shared something deep and bonding in working together to care for Ian and to see him talk again.

Ian slipped off the couch and ran over to hug Graham's leg.

"Thanks, little buddy." Graham's eyes glazed, and his voice was thick with emotion. He kneeled and gave Ian a hug.

She rose from the couch. He stood up from hugging Ian and opened his arms to embrace her. "Take care of yourself, Graham." She relished the warmth of his arms before he pulled away.

His eyes were still glazed as he touched her chin, offering her a faint quick smile before walking across the room and opening the door that led to the garage.

His leaving was a reminder that the bond she felt toward him was temporary. Wrestling with a sense of loss, she stared out the window from across the room. She didn't want him to go.

She stepped a little closer to the window, watching Graham backing the car out of the garage. Then she frowned. Something was wrong.

Graham had stopped the car halfway down the driveway with the engine still running.

From where he sat behind the wheel, Graham didn't like the looks of the blue compact car that eased down the street, slowing even more as it passed the house where Marielle and Ian were. The car turned a corner at the end of the block.

He waited for a moment while his car idled, half expecting to see the other vehicle coming back the way it had gone. Though she was standing a safe distance away from the window, he could see

Marielle staring out at him with questioning look on her face. Seeing her stabbed at his heart. Going back to his job had never been so hard.

Officer Phelps had risen to look out the window as well.

Satisfied that his suspicions had been unwarranted, he shifted into Reverse. He waved at Officer Phelps and then checked his rearview mirror. He'd backed up only a few feet when he saw the blue car again. It had circled the block and was coming up the street again.

Still halfway down the driveway, he killed the engine and jumped out. The blue car sped up. Adrenaline surged through his body as he ran toward the house.

Officer Phelps swung the door open just as Graham reached for the knob.

"I saw," said Phelps.

Two gunshots shattered the front window. Graham caught a glimpse of the blue car whizzing by just before he stepped across the threshold, dropped to the floor and kicked the door shut with his foot.

Marielle gathered Ian up and retreated toward the first-floor bedroom. Officer O'Brian swooped down the stairs with her gun drawn.

More shots, this time aimed at the side of the house, resounded through the air. Marielle emerged from the bedroom still holding Ian. She dropped down to the floor.

"They shot through the bedroom window." Her voice was frantic.

There had to be at least two shooters. To take the shot at the side of the house, one must have gotten out of the car. They were surrounded.

Officer Phelps addressed the policewoman. "I'll take care of these guys. You get them out of here."

O'Brian signaled to Marielle and Graham. "The patrol car in the garage. Come on, let's go."

As they retreated toward the door that

led to the attached garage, Graham heard Officer Phelps calling for backup. Graham wrapped his arm around Marielle and guided her into the garage. He opened the back door of the car for her and Ian to get in while Officer O'Brian slipped behind the wheel.

Marielle lay across the back seat, drawing Ian close to her. Graham got into the front passenger seat with his gun drawn. Officer O'Brian held the garage door remote in her hand. She pressed the button and the door began to rise.

It was halfway up when she pressed it again. A quick glance over his shoulder told him that the blue car was going by. More shots filled the air. A bullet pinged when it hit the metal of the garage door just as it closed.

Craning his neck, he stared at the garage door. The threat of danger seemed to electrify the air around him. Resting on her side, Marielle stirred in the back seat. Her coat made a rustling noise as she drew Ian closer to her stomach.

He turned his attention to the front seat.

The hand O'Brian held the remote in was shaking.

"Here." Graham reached for the remote. "You focus on driving. I'll let you know when the coast is clear."

Graham pushed the remote. The door eased up. Because it was a double garage with a wide driveway, she'd be able to get around the car he'd left halfway up the driveway. While still looking over his shoulder, he crouched in his seat, trying to get a view of the street. "It's clear."

This time, she backed out even before the door was completely open.

As soon as O'Brian had the vehicle clear of the garage door, he pressed the remote to close it.

Officer O'Brian backed up out onto the street, twisting the wheel as she gained speed.

Graham continued to scan the area

around him and behind him as their vehicle zoomed up the street. Two police cars whizzed past them. The cars split off in different directions as they got close to the safe house. Phelps must have called for more officers.

"I'm going to head toward the highway for now," said Officer O'Brian. "It'll be easier to spot a tail and lose them if we need to."

Marielle's voice floated up from the back seat. "Isn't there someplace we can take Ian so he's safe?"

His throat grew tight at the vision of Marielle holding Ian close. They both looked so vulnerable.

His voice came out as a soft whisper. "It kind of depends on if they catch these guys or not." Graham turned fully around in the seat, so he was looking through the windshield. He addressed his comment to O'Brian. "Don't you think?"

"Yes, we'll have to wait to hear." Officer O'Brian reached the edge of town and took an exit for the highway. "Once we're sure that we're not being followed, we can go back to the police station, maybe, as a temporary measure. Phelps is in charge of protection duty. He'll let me know our next move."

Both Graham and Officer O'Brian watched the cars around them. Hopefully, the arrival of the police cars scared the men in the blue compact into getting away rather than coming after them. No doubt, it was Georgio and Eric who had come for them once again.

The car radio crackled. She lifted it from the receiver. "O'Brian here."

Phelps's voice came through. "Perpetrators still at large. They abandoned the blue compact. No sign of them fleeing on foot. We think they must have had a backup car close by."

Graham tensed. That meant they no longer knew what the shooters were driving. They could be in any of the cars on this highway.

"Got it," said O'Brian. "What's our next step?"

"You can't bring them back to the safe house," said Phelps. "This place is compromised."

"Should we head toward the police station?"

"I'm concerned that it is too obvious a choice and that the suspects might be waiting and watching for your arrival."

"So what are you suggesting?" O'Brian let up on the talk button.

"My brother is a manager at the Big Sky Hotel," said Phelps. "I can make a call."

"I know which one you're talking about," said O'Brian.

"He'll let you in the back and escort you up the service elevator until we can figure out something more permanent. His name is Dane Phelps. I'll text you his cell phone number. I'll get to the hotel as fast as I can to provide the additional protection needed."

"Ten-four," said O'Brian. She placed the radio back in its slot and stared out at the road. "I got to get turned around here."

While O'Brian concentrated on getting to the hotel, Graham remained alert to the traffic around them. Being in the police vehicle made it too easy for them to be tracked, but they had no choice at this point.

When Officer O'Brian took the exit that led back into town, several other cars followed them.

Graham couldn't shake the tension that had wrapped around his chest, making it hard to get a deep breath.

Once on city streets again, O'Brian slowed down.

"How far away are we?"

"It's the other side of town," said O'Brian.

"Why don't I make the call to the hotel, so the guy is waiting for us when we get there?"

O'Brian pulled her cell phone from her shirt pocket and unlocked it. "That would be great. Check my text messages for Officer Phelps's text."

City businesses in buildings close together opened up to fields and warehouses farther apart. The hotel must be at the edge of town.

Looking down as he focused on the phone, he pressed in the number and waited while the phone rang. He lifted his head just in time to see a car fill his field of vision as it crashed into the passenger side door.

SEVENTEEN

Upon impact, the whole car shook, causing Marielle to mash her teeth together as her heart raced. She wrapped her arms even tighter around Ian. Though she wanted to see what was going on, her instinct told her to stay hidden.

O'Brian shifted into Reverse and backed the police car up. Graham had grabbed the radio calling for backup. He held his gun in his other hand.

A bullet hit the car as O'Brian backed up at a high speed.

She let go of Ian. "Get down on the floor. Stay flat."

The boy rolled away from her onto the carpeted floor of the back seat.

Graham lifted his gun and shot several

times through the rolled-down window, ducking low after each shot.

There was another crash and the crunch of metal, this time toward the front of the car. O'Brian shifted as the car made a grinding noise but did not move. Graham jumped out.

She winced at the volley of gunfire she heard.

Oh God, let him not get shot.

She placed her hand on Ian's back.

The next few seconds went by in a blur. Glass shattered above her, spraying over her. She heard the clicks of the door locks opening. The driver's side door opened, as did the back passenger door close to her feet.

Hands like iron clamped around her ankles and dragged her out. She heard the sound of men punching each other and had only a flashing image of Ian's blond head as he was gathered into someone's arms.

She gasped and reached out toward him.

Ian cried out, "Mari."

A hood was put over her head, and she was dragged a short distance. Her captor had wrapped his arm around her.

She heard a voice say, "Come closer and I'll kill her."

Something hard pressed against her skull. A gun?

She was shoved onto a hard surface. She heard the squeal of tires. The car started to move. In the distance, sirens wailed.

She could feel the car rolling, gaining speed.

What had happened to Ian?

She reached to pull the hood off her head.

Hands wrapped around her wrists, drawing them together and binding them with what felt like rope behind her back. She could hear the man's heavy breathing as he secured the rope.

Her stomach pressed against the hard surface of the car.

The car seemed to go even faster, jostling her, and it sounded like the surface of the road had changed from smooth concrete to gravel.

She could hear voices.

"She's not going anywhere," said the first voice. That sounded like Eric Smith.

"Make the call," said the second man, and she guessed that must be Georgio Franks.

A few seconds passed, and then Eric said, "This is a message for the cops holding Ian Roane. I think we have something you want. We'll trade her for the boy. You have one hour."

As her cheek pressed against the floor, Marielle's breaths were shallow and rapid, causing the hood to move in and out against her face. She feared she would hyperventilate.

Come on, Marielle, hold it together.

The call must have gone into the police department unless the men had somehow figured out Graham's number.

At least this meant that Ian was safe. Graham must have been able to grab him before the men did. They did not know that Ian had already identified Georgio as Kristen's killer, and they must have thought they could still prevent it from happening.

She knew Graham would not put Ian at risk. It was up to her to figure out how to escape.

The two men were playing a desperate game. She was pretty sure they would shoot her if they didn't get what they wanted and fast. The whole thing might be a ruse, to buy them time to flee the country. They had to know that the police wouldn't hand a child over to them. How smart were they? Was it possible this was a plot to distract the police while they plotted a way to get at Ian?

She didn't know what they were up to. She only knew she had to get away.

She tried to draw her hands apart. She'd

been bound with something that had a little give to it. A bungee cord maybe.

The back end of the car slanted downward. They were going up a hill then down the other side. The car continued for a few more minutes and then came to a stop. She heard doors opening and being slammed. The air around her grew quiet. Her heart raced. Both men must have gotten out of the car. She lifted her head, trying to push herself up.

The hood was not secured. She worked her way up to her knees and bent her head while shaking it to get the hood to come off. The car was in a lot of what looked like and defunct business surrounded by open fields. There was another metal building not too far away that looked like it was not in use either, judging from the pileup of snow and overgrown vegetation.

She was in the cargo area of an SUV. The back hatch swung open. The short bald man, Eric, shook his head.

He grinned in a sinister way. Only one

side of his mouth curled up. "Trying to get smart with me, huh?"

He grabbed her arm painfully at the elbow, forcing her to move toward him. The hood went back over her head.

"Put your feet on the ground," said Eric. When she hesitated, he jerked her arm so it hurt. She complied. He controlled her by clamping his hand around her elbow and squeezing if she moved the wrong way. Her boots stepped across the hard surface. Out of the bottom of the hood, she could see cracked concrete.

A door slid open and she was pushed inside. It grew even darker, though she could still feel a slight breeze. She was shoved to the ground. Her bound hands touched cold concrete. The odor of oil and dirt hung in the air.

The men shuffled around for several minutes. Then she felt her feet being lifted and something being wound around her ankles.

"This ought to keep them busy while we get out of here," Eric said.

Georgio laughed.

Eric pulled the hood off her head and shoved a gag into her mouth. It tasted like dirt.

Eric patted her cheek. "Now no one can hear you scream for help."

Georgio waited a few feet away. Eric moved to join him.

Her view was partially obstructed by a piece of farm equipment. She could hear the men's footfalls on the concrete. A door creaked shut and a few minutes later a car engine started up.

As the noise of the car faded, she focused on her surroundings. She was inside a metal building with broken, rusty-looking farm equipment, wood pallets and some barrels. The metal exterior of the building had holes in it where the wind blew through and light got in.

If she could get her hands free, she could reach her phone in her coat pocket to tell Graham where she was. The men hadn't thought to take it from her. She twisted her wrists in and out, trying to create more give in the bungee cord. The icky-tasting gag pressed against her tongue.

She was able to move one hand an inch or so though it remained restrained.

As she struggled, her breath came out in rapid shallow bursts. Then another sound became apparent. She stopped struggling and sat up straight. Where was the noise coming from? She recognized it as the rhythmic tick of a clock.

Her hands stilled. She looked to one side and then the other. It took her a second to process what she was seeing. When she did, blood froze in her veins. Off to one side was a clock attached to a bomb set to go off in less than ten minutes.

Graham looked at the GPS map on his phone while Officer Zetler drove the patrol car. There were three possible directions the men could have gone after taking Marielle. He'd made sure Ian was with Officer O'Brian, who would take him to the hotel where he'd be safe, and then Graham had jumped in the police car with one of the other officers. Though all had headed in the direction they'd seen the culprits' car go, each one of the three police cars had taken off in a different direction once the road forked.

The GPS showed no structures in the area. Through the windshield, he saw fields of snow-covered grass and gravel roads with a few clusters of trees.

"Doesn't look like there's anything out this way," said Officer Zetler.

Graham's heart sank. "You're probably right. No one else had radioed that they've seen anything either. We might as well keep looking."

They passed a concrete pad that must have had a building on it at one time.

The police officer pressed the gas as

they climbed a hill. When they came down on the other side of it, he saw two metal buildings not too far apart. Neither looked like they were in use.

The first building had large garage doors. This might be a good hiding place for a car.

"Let's stop and search here," said Graham.

The officer nodded and grabbed his radio. "Be advised. We have stopped at an abandoned warehouse on Old Fork Road. Will execute a search."

The two men got out with their weapons drawn and made their way toward the door. Graham reached for the knob. It creaked as he opened it. The men slipped inside and pressed against opposite walls.

Graham scanned the room. Disappointment washed over him. There was no car inside.

"I guess that's a wash." He moved back toward the door.

A noise emanated from the other side

of a piece of farm equipment, a sort of strange groaning.

Both men lifted their guns and moved in from opposite sides.

Graham traversed the concrete floor and swung around the old combine. He holstered his gun as a cavalcade of emotions whirled through him at what he saw. He was overjoyed to find Marielle alive but angry at the two men for having so obviously mistreated her. His relief at seeing Marielle was washed away by how frantic she appeared as she tried to say something despite being gagged. Her eyes were wide with fear as she shook her head back and forth.

He kneeled and reached up to remove the gag.

"Bomb." She tilted her head off to the side.

He followed the direction she indicated and froze in disbelief as reality sank in. They had seconds to get out of here before it went off.

He scooped her up in his arms as he yelled at the other officer. "Bomb. Go now." Slowed by carrying Marielle, he lagged behind Officer Zetler as he opened the door that led outside. The other officer stood holding the door open for them.

Graham had just reached the threshold when a blast of heat and a force like a weight being thrown at his back hit him. The explosion pushed them the remaining distance through the door and out onto the gravel.

He kept his arms around Marielle as they fell to the ground. Debris rained down on their heads. It had not been a powerful bomb, though if they had remained inside, they would not have survived.

The other officer shook Graham's shoulder. His mouth moved, forming the words, *Are you okay?*

He'd temporarily lost his hearing. Graham nodded.

Graham turned to face Marielle, touching his hand to her cheek. "You okay?" His voice sounded strange through his hearing loss. His ears felt like they were plugged, as if he'd been on a long plane flight. He reached to untie her hands.

She nodded. "They were just here ten minutes ago."

His hearing was coming back. Though she must be experiencing it too because she shouted when she spoke.

He undid the bungee cord that secured her hands.

Officer Zetler spoke up. "I'll radio the other patrol cars, so they know where to search." He ran back to the police car.

Once her hands were free, Marielle helped Graham get the rope off her ankles.

"We can still catch them. We're the closest." Her voice was hoarse.

"We need to get you to a hospital. Both of us should be checked out," he said. He didn't have any broken bones. He'd be fine. He'd been through worse. At least his head hadn't been injured this time. It was Marielle he was worried about. Not just her physical well-being concerned him. He wasn't sure what she'd been through with the kidnappers.

"That can wait. I'm just a little shaken is all." She leaned closer to him. "We can get these guys."

"You need to be checked out. That has to be my priority."

She gripped his coat. "The man who killed Ian's mother is going to try to get away, to leave the country."

He looked around. There was only one road that led away from the property. Only one direction the men could have gone unless they doubled back the way they'd come, which he doubted they would do. Too much chance of running into the police.

Officer Zetler had jumped into the patrol car and was rolling toward them. Graham helped Marielle get to her feet. His arms were still around her as he assisted her into the back seat of the police vehicle. She was still weak and shaken from what she'd been through.

He slipped into the passenger seat.

"The other two cars are on route to the intersection where this road meets the main road," said the officer.

"They're probably going to try to go to the nearest airport." Marielle spoke from the back seat. Her voice still sounded weak.

Graham glanced back at her and she offered him a soft smile. "The both of us should probably be checked out by a doctor."

"Got it," said Officer Zetler. They were headed in the same direction that the men must have escaped in. "There's an urgent care on the edge of town."

They drove for several miles down the gravel road. A few houses came into view along with a barn and a field full of cows. He could see the outskirts of town in the distance.

The radio crackled.

Officer Zetler picked up the radio. "Go ahead."

"We were waiting for him at the crossroad where the pavement starts. Thought I had hidden the patrol car well enough, but the suspect must have seen us. He did an unexpected U-turn. I'm in pursuit."

Officer Zetler adjusted the radio in his hand. "You mean the car turned back the way he came?"

"Yes." The voice of the other officer came through the radio.

That meant the car was coming toward them. He scanned the road and the area around them, not seeing the car anywhere.

Marielle sat up and leaned forward, gripping the headrest of the front passenger seat.

Graham kept searching as his heart pounded. He glanced at his GPS map. While there were side roads the men could have taken to access the farms and houses in the area, those roads didn't lead anywhere.

Officer Zetler increased his speed. He too was scanning the entire countryside.

"There, over by that red house." Marielle pointed through the windshield.

The car was traveling at a high rate of speed. It looked like the dark-colored SUV that had rammed them.

"I see it." Officer Zetler zoomed ahead and then took a tight turn to get on the side road.

Graham noticed the name of the road as the sign whizzed by.

Graham got on the radio and let the other policeman know where they were going. "We just turned onto Heebs Road. It looks like they're headed toward the forest."

"10-4. I'll get there as fast as I can."

Once the SUV turned into the trees, Graham lost sight of it.

They traveled up the dirt road that was surrounded by snow-covered trees on both sides. Graham leaned forward, hoping to see the SUV.

The road grew rougher and harder to navigate as they came to a hill. Down below was the SUV, pulled off to one side. He could not tell if the men were inside.

They radioed the other car to let the officer know what they'd found.

A voice came through the radio. "I just turned on the mountain road. Should be there soon."

Officer Zetler rolled the car forward until he was a few yards behind the dark SUV.

Graham unclicked his seat belt. "Marielle, you stay in the car."

The two men got out and approached the car with their weapons drawn.

EIGHTEEN

Marielle rose from the back seat and reached into the front driver's side so she could lock the doors.

After sitting back down, she watched as Graham and Officer Zetler peered inside the car and then opened the two front doors and the back hatch, shaking their heads.

Another patrol car joined them.

Officer Zetler leaned into the driver's side of the SUV and then spoke over his shoulder radio. She heard him through the radio in the car. "Looks like they ran out of gas."

A voice from the other patrol car answered, "They couldn't have gotten far. I'll drive up ahead and search on foot."

Then Officer Zetler radioed the third patrol car to come aid in the search and signed off.

The second patrol car circled around the vehicle she was in and then parked ahead of the SUV. With their weapons drawn, Graham and Officer Zetler had already headed into the forest close to where the SUV had been abandoned.

While she watched the dark forest, Marielle waited and listened. The radio crackled again when one of the officers called for another patrol car and a helicopter to help with the search.

The silence seemed to hold an unnamed tension. She studied the trees on one side of the car and then cast her attention to the view out the back window.

Glass shattered around her. Her hands jerked up to protect her face.

The driver's side window had been shot out.

Georgio was at the door, reaching his

hand in to unlock the car. Eric got into the passenger seat.

Marielle's heart pounded as she moved to open the back door. The cold barrel of a gun pressed against her temple.

"Oh no you don't, you're collateral." Eric grinned. "Sit down, sweetie."

Georgio had already started the car and was rolling forward. Graham emerged from the forest and raised his gun as the blond man sped up. He fired a shot, but the stolen police car just went faster. It must not have hit anything.

She could see the other patrol car pulled off the road but no sign of the other officer, who was probably deep in the forest.

Eric still held his gun pointed in her direction, though he had half turned around in his seat. She glanced over her shoulder to see Officer Zetler emerging from the trees.

A conversation came through the radio. The voice was Officer Zetler's. "Suspects have taken patrol car. Headed in your direction."

"Got it, I'll head back to the road," came the response from the officer still hidden in the forest.

"That's sweet," Georgio spoke as he tapped the radio. "We get to know exactly what their plans are."

Eric didn't seem as relaxed as the blond man. He glanced ahead and then peered through the back window. "Maybe get turned around, huh? Those two cops behind us can't catch us on foot. We don't know where this road ends up. It might be a dead end."

Fear skittered across her nerves as Marielle studied the forest. No one else emerged through the trees. Where were the other police officers?

Georgio stopped the car and backed up, trying to get turned around on the narrow road. It took three times of backing up and pulling forward before the car was pointed back the way the men had come.

The car had just started to gain speed when three shots were fired from outside the vehicle.

Before ducking down, Marielle caught a glimpse of Graham moving through the trees. How fast must he have been running to get into place to make the shots?

The car jerked and lurched before stopping. Georgio pressed the gas but the car moved only a few feet.

"Shot the tires out." Eric pushed open the door and took off running toward the trees.

Marielle reached for the door handle on the side where she'd seen Graham.

Georgio exited from the driver's seat, flung open her door and grabbed her by her hair. The pain forced her to crawl out toward him and stand up. The blond man held a gun to her temple while still pulling her hair with his other hand.

Graham's voice came through the trees, though she couldn't see where he was hidden. "Let her go."

Georgio jerked the back of her head. He stood behind her, using her body as a shield. He remained close to the dead patrol car to shield his back. "Let me go and she's all yours."

The wind blew through the treetops, but Graham remained silent and hidden. What was he planning? Where was Officer Zetler?

Off to the side, she heard gunshots. Eric stood at the edge of the forest holding a gun. The other patrol car had stopped. The windshield was shattered. She could not see the officer behind the wheel. Had he been killed by the gunfire?

Eric advanced on the car with his gun held up.

Georgio pulled her toward the working patrol car but stopped so the defunct patrol car still provided his back with cover. She knew if she tried to get away, he would shoot her.

She watched in horror as the short man opened the driver's side door and pulled the police officer out. The officer clutched his chest where a patch of red was spreading. He fell on the ground. Eric kicked him and took his gun when the officer reached for it. He got behind the wheel and drove toward Georgio.

Her stomach roiled, and it felt like she might throw up. She had to do something. Graham must be watching and waiting for a chance to get at Georgio without killing her. This was the man who had killed Kristen and Charlie and tried to kill David. He was not going to get away, not if she could help it.

The working patrol car edged close to where Georgio stood.

She elbowed the blond man in the stomach. His back slammed against the car. He still held her hair, but the hard butt of the gun no longer pressed against her head.

Eric was feet away from them in the stolen patrol car. She could hear the engine humming.

She twisted to get away, putting a few inches between herself and Georgio even though he still held her by the hair. A gunshot was fired, not close to her.

She couldn't see what had happened.

Georgio let go of her and ran toward the working patrol car.

Graham burst from behind a tree. He held her in his arms for only a second. "Get down."

She slipped behind him, dropped to her stomach and crawled toward the cover of a nearby tree. The trunk shielded her as she kneeled.

Three gunshots spaced a few seconds apart filled the air. She squeezed her eyes shut and prayed that Graham and Officer Zetler had not been hit.

NINETEEN

While Graham had been trying to free Marielle, Officer Zetler had been advancing on the working patrol car, looking for his chance to get at Eric who sat behind the wheel. He'd fired a shot but had been too far away to hit with any accuracy.

Georgio, who was feet away from getting into the passenger side of the patrol car with Eric at the wheel, lifted his gun and fired at Graham, who ducked behind the vehicle with the blown tires. His heart pounded. A door slammed and the patrol car rolled forward.

He had to stop these men before they got away.

Officer Zetler chased the car as it gained speed.

Graham stepped free from the shelter of the disabled car as the other car rolled by. He could see Eric in the driver's seat. He lifted his gun and aimed at the tires.

He ran out in pursuit of the car as it continued to roll forward. Georgio leaned out the window of the front passenger side shooting at Officer Zetler, forcing him to hang back and take cover.

Graham kept running, staying closer to the driver's side. Through the windows, he saw that Officer Zetler was still advancing with his weapon aimed in one hand while he held a bloody arm close to his body. A bullet had hit him.

Graham shot again at the tires. The car slowed but kept rolling. He caught up to the car, reaching for the driver's side door handle. He flung the door open with one hand and lifted his gun in the other. Eric leaned out of the car and grabbed Graham's wrist, bending it back so the gun was pointed upward. The short man reached with the other hand and knocked the gun free of Graham's grip.

Graham lunged to grab Eric with both hands. The car had stopped altogether. Graham pulled the driver from behind the wheel.

The man punched him across the jaw. Pain vibrated through his head. Wherever his gun had fallen, Eric had not had time to grab it. A shot was fired from within the cab of the vehicle. Georgio was trying to shoot Graham. It sounded like the bullet had ricocheted inside the car.

He wrestled the short man out of his seat as Eric hit him several times several times in the stomach and head. When he reached to get Eric in a chokehold, he was struck hard across the jaw, leaving him momentarily stunned.

Eric took off running. Graham sprinted after him and tackled him. He continued to fight even as he lay on his stomach.

Graham shouted, "DEA. You're under arrest."

The man finally stopped fighting and grew still. Holding the man in place, Graham lifted his head in time to see Marielle burst out from her hiding place and run to the other side of the car.

He called out her name.

What was she doing putting herself in danger like that?

When Marielle saw that Officer Zetler was injured, she knew she had to do something. Georgio was not getting away. She wanted him in jail. She wanted justice for all the pain he'd caused.

Officer Zetler was bent over but still holding his gun. Georgio had been preoccupied with trying to stop Graham but now had slipped into the driver's seat. She heard gears shift as she took Officer Zetler's gun and ran up to the passenger side window.

Georgio pressed the gas but on two flat tires he couldn't get much traction on the dirt road. She came to the passenger side window and held the gun up.

"Stop right there." She lifted the gun with trembling hands.

Georgio sneered at her and reached for the gun he'd set on the console.

Adrenaline surged through her. "Don't even try it." She fired a shot directly into the seat cushion.

Georgio winced at the noise and held up his hands. "You got me."

She relaxed a little, but the gun still shook.

Georgio pushed open the driver's side door and tumbled out. He dropped to his knees. She couldn't see him anymore from the passenger side.

She heard a voice on the other side of the car. "I don't think so. Not today." It was Graham.

When she circled around to the other side of the car, she saw Officer Zetler leaning over Eric, handcuffing him. Graham held a muddy gun on Georgio.

She heard the sound of a helicopter. The other injured police officer still lay on the ground up the road.

"We need to tell that chopper to land so it can transport these two injured officers," she said.

Still clutching his arm, Officer Zetler rose to his feet and reached into the patrol car to use the radio.

Graham kept his gun on Georgio.

When she peered down the road, she saw that the third patrol car was on its way. Within minutes, the chopper found a place to land and the two injured police officers were secured inside. The patrol officer in the third car handcuffed Georgio, placing him and Eric in the back of his car.

Marielle and Graham stood beside the patrol car she'd been held captive in. The officer approached them. "I radioed for three tow trucks. You can catch a ride with one of the drivers."

Graham raised his hand in acknowledgment as she murmured a thank-you.

The patrol car with the perpetrators in the back drove past them, turning around when the road got wide enough to do so without slipping off.

The officer at the wheel waved to them as the car went by headed down the mountain road.

Georgio sneered at her from the back seat, sending shivers down her spine.

Unrepentant. How could a person get to that level of evil?

Snow began to fall as she let out a heavy breath. "I guess it's over. It doesn't quite feel real to me."

Graham stood close enough to her that their shoulders touched. "I understand the feeling." He reached for her hand and held it for a long moment. "You were brave back there. I know that was scary holding the gun on a criminal and firing it."

"I just didn't want him to get away after all the evil he was responsible for." A heaviness fell around her. She wouldn't be seeing Graham much longer now that Kristen's killer had been caught. "Do you think Ian is safe now?"

"Yes, this was personal to Georgio. He didn't want Ian to identify him. I doubt other cartel members would want to expend resources on coming after the boy," said Graham. "As a distributor, Georgio is not high ranking and easy to replace."

"Thank you for helping Ian have a shot at a decent life." Marielle took in a deep breath. "Guess you'll be going wherever your job takes you next?"

"There's a few things I need to do to wrap this case up first."

He had not yet let go of her hand. She relished the warmth and strength of his touch, feeling like there was something more she wanted to say but not knowing how to say it. The same feelings from ten years ago bombarded her. Her life would seem emptier without him. Just as it had in the past, it would take time to adjust to the loss.

The first tow truck appeared on the road below.

Graham squeezed her fingers before letting go.

They waited while the driver got the first car hooked up and then climbed into the cab with him. Marielle sat in the middle between the two men.

"Where am I dropping you folks off at?"

"I need to go to the Big Sky Hotel. There's a little boy I want to give a hug to." Ian's life would no longer be under threat, though his future was unsure. They still didn't know how David was doing or what he would be charged with. Whatever the outcome, she vowed to remain in the boy's life in whatever capacity she could. "He and I will be able to go back to my home...for now."

"I'll go with you to the hotel," said Graham. "I'd like to see the little guy one more time."

One more time. His words echoed through her head and filled her with sadness.

As the snow hit the windshield and the two men engaged in small talk, she realized that she'd fallen in love with Graham all over again. But she wasn't about to say anything. The pain of him leaving would be even worse this time. They'd both been immature when they were first engaged. She'd fallen even deeper in love with the courageous and compassionate man Graham had become.

When the tow truck driver pulled into the parking lot of the hotel and let Graham and Marielle out, Graham felt a tightening in his chest he didn't understand.

They stepped into the lobby where Officer O'Brian waited holding Ian's hand.

Marielle held her arms out and bent down. "There's my guy." Ian ran to her.

"Suspects in custody. A good day's work, huh?" said O'Brian to Graham.

"Yes, it's good, but two officers were injured in the process." Graham's attention was on Marielle as she held Ian and pressed her head close to his.

Ian pointed down a hallway. "They have ice cream here."

There was something stunning about hearing Ian speak a complete sentence. Marielle raised her eyebrows, and her face glowed when she looked in Graham's direction. Together, they had given Ian back his voice.

"Why don't you show me?" Marielle put Ian down and took his hand. She headed up the hallway with a backward glance at Graham.

The look on her face warmed his heart.

The tightness in his chest increased when he could no longer see them. What was that about?

O'Brian grabbed his arm. "David didn't make it. He died about an hour ago."

Feeling numb, he let the news sink in. "Ian's an orphan. Marielle doesn't know?"

"I sent her a text when it happened. I didn't want to say anything in front of Ian."

To his knowledge, she had not checked her phone in the last hour. "I think I'll go join them. Thank you for watching over Ian."

Officer O'Brian stood with her hands on her hips. "When you're ready, I can give you all a ride to wherever you need to go?"

"Sounds good."

He hurried down the hallway and into the restaurant. Marielle and Ian were sitting opposite each other in a corner booth. Only a few other people were eating at this hour.

A smile spread across Ian's face, and

he put his arms up in the air. "Graham's here."

He still couldn't get used to the sound of that sweet voice.

Ian scooted over and patted the seat by him.

He sat down.

"We've already ordered." He saw a sort of darkness in her eyes despite the lilt in her voice. Her phone sat on the table. She knew David had not made it.

"I'll give you bites of mine." Ian spoke as he tugged on Graham's sleeve.

"That's awfully nice of you to share, little buddy." His gaze rested on Marielle. "You checked your texts?"

She nodded. He wanted to ask her more. Would she be adopting Ian and raising him as a single mother? But that wasn't a conversation to have in front of the boy.

The bowls of ice cream were placed on the table. Marielle asked for an extra spoon for Graham. Ian laughed while they ate the ice cream together. Marielle scooted her bowl across the table too so he could taste her blueberry ice cream.

The waiter brought the check for them when they'd finished. He stood for a moment with his hands at his side. "Did you enjoy your ice cream?"

All three of them nodded.

"You three have a great day. You have a very nice little family here."

Marielle locked Graham in her gaze for an intense moment. Is that what they looked like to the world, a family?

They found Officer O'Brian and got into her car. Graham sat in the front seat with Marielle and Ian in the back.

"Where to?"

Where was he going? He had a report to write and he needed to check in with his handler, but where was he going? Where did he belong?

"Ian and I get to go home. Eighteen Eleven Maverick Lane."

"Okay. And then, Graham, do you want to go back to the police station with me?"

"I guess so." His things were still back at Bridger Bible Camp. He'd have to go up there eventually.

O'Brian drove out of town and up a country road to the two-story house with trees on one side of it.

"This is it. My place." Marielle unbuckled her seat belt.

Ian's soft voice floated up to his ear from the back seat. "Is Graham coming with us?"

Graham turned to look at the blond boy as he stuck his fingers in his mouth. The request made the tightness in his chest return.

"Marielle, do you want me to help you and Ian get settled in?"

"Sure." Her voice was faint, and she had said the word almost as if it was a question.

"I can send a car around to get you in a bit," said O'Brian.

"Sounds good," said Graham.

The three of them walked toward the

door with Ian in the middle. Ian took Graham's hand. He was already holding Marielle's.

Once inside, Marielle spoke to Ian. "Why don't you go to your room and find a toy that Graham might want to see?"

"Or we can do a puzzle." He scrambled up the stairs and disappeared.

Graham spoke up. "With David gone, are you going to adopt Ian?"

"I'm going to do everything I can to try to make that happen." She stepped toward him, eyes fixed on him. "What's going on? Why didn't you just go to the police station?"

His mouth had gone dry. "I'm having a hard time saying goodbye…to Ian."

"I think he will be confused when you go. I'm glad you're being sensitive to that. But you shouldn't drag it out too long."

"I care about that kid."

"That makes it hard, doesn't it…to leave again." She looked off to the side and ran her fingers through her hair. "Maybe you can come back for visits."

"I'm not sure I want to leave. I'm just so confused." He massaged his chest where the muscles were taut.

"What are you talking about?"

"When I left last time, I thought I was doing you a favor. I was the only Christian in my family, and you had this long heritage of faith. I had a terrible father and no male role models. You had strong, loving parents. You deserved someone who was more solid."

She stepped toward him and grabbed his arms above the elbow. "Why should any of that matter? I never looked at you and thought that. What I was drawn to was *your* faith. There are no grandchildren in God's kingdom."

"I never thought of it that way." He looked into her eyes. "When we started talking about having children, I was afraid that I would be just like my father. You deserved better."

"I wanted to marry you, Graham." Her eyes searched his as she shook her head. "Something's changed though. You said you were confused."

"It's not just that I care about Ian. I love him. I didn't think I could ever feel that for a kid. I don't just want to visit. I want to be a part of his life and I want to be with you." He took a step back and put his hand over his heart. He knew then what the tightness in his chest was about. "I love Ian and I love you and I want us to be a family together."

Once he'd spoken the words, the tension eased from his chest and he knew that what he said was true.

"But your job. The travel and excitement, the sense of purpose."

"I used to love what I did, but losing Cesar made me think about doing something less stressful and not as heartbreaking. I want to be here in Montana with you and Ian. Marielle, will you marry me?"

Light came into her eyes as her face filled with joy. "Oh, Graham, yes."

He gathered her into his arms. "I will never leave you again. I promise." He bent his head and kissed her.

He felt pressure against his leg and looked down to find Ian holding a stuffed animal and hugging his thigh.

Marielle laughed.

Graham reached down and took Ian into his arms. Marielle wrapped her arm around his back and pressed close to him.

Joy burst through him. He kissed Marielle again, realizing he was with the two people he wanted to spend the rest of his life with.

EPILOGUE

As Graham took her hand and turned toward the minister, Marielle glanced around at the crowd gathered to watch them be married. All the people she loved were here with her today.

Her mom and dad and sisters smiled. Her whole family had extended such love and acceptance to both Ian and Graham. Graham's new co-workers, the other officers of the Clarksville police force, had shown up in uniform. His job with the city police would be a lot less stressful and keep him close to home.

She glanced out the window of the sanctuary of Bridger Bible Camp at the expanse of blue sky. What a perfect summer day.

"Please turn to face each other," said the minister.

Graham took both her hands in his as they said their vows. With each promise they repeated to each other she saw the light of love shining in his eyes.

She was so lost in Graham's eyes she barely heard the minister speak. "You may present each other with your ring."

Graham turned and crouched next to Ian, who held the pillow with the rings on it. The boy offered Marielle a mischievous smile. They had a long road ahead with Ian, but he was smiling…and talking much more these days.

Graham took the rings, leaning to whisper in Ian's ear. "Thanks, little buddy."

Ian swayed back and forth, his face glowing.

After they placed the rings on each other's fingers, the minister announced, "Ladies and gentlemen, may I present to you Mr. and Mrs. Flynn."

Music played as people applauded, and

they headed down the aisle. The doors burst open. They stepped outside surrounded by the mountains she loved in the place that meant so much to both her and Graham.

She couldn't wait to start her life together with Graham as her husband and Ian as their son.

It truly was a beautiful day.

* * * * *

*If you enjoyed this story,
check out other titles by Sharon Dunn
available now on LoveInspired.com!*

Dear Reader,

Thank you so much for going along for the wild ride and intense danger that Graham and Marielle faced as they sought to protect Ian and each other. As I wrote their love story, I thought a great deal about God's timing. Though they loved each other when they were young, Marielle and Graham had to mature and experience some loss before they were truly ready to commit to each other. I recently listened to a sermon that said none of our suffering or loss is ever wasted. God's timing is always perfect as well in terms of when we have seasons of sorrow and times of joy. I know for me these last years have been a time of growing to trust God in terms of what He allows into my life. Sometimes the loss and suffering doesn't make sense right away. Whatever you are experiencing today, be it joy or sorrow, I hope you will lean into God's comfort and His provision. I love to hear from readers. Please contact me through my website at www.sharon-dunnbooks.net.

Sharon Dunn